PENGUIN BOOKS

FRENCH LEAVE

P. G. Wodehouse was born in Guildford in 1881 and educated at Dulwich College. After working for the Hong Kong and Shanghai Bank for two years, he left to earn his living as a journalist and storywriter, writing the 'By the Way' column in the old *Globe*. He also contributed a series of school stories to a magazine for boys, the *Captain*, in one of which Psmith made his first appearance. Going to America before the First World War, he sold a serial to the *Saturday Evening Post*, and for the next twenty-five years almost all his books appeared first in this magazine. He was part author and writer of the lyrics of eighteen musical comedies, including *Kissing Time*. He married in 1914 and in 1955 took American citizenship. He wrote over ninety books, and his work has won world-wide acclaim, having been translated into many languages. *The Times* hailed him as a 'comic genius recognized in his lifetime as a classic and an old master of farce'.

P. G. Wodehouse said, 'I believe there are two ways of writing novels. One is mine, making a sort of musical comedy without music and ignoring real life altogether; the other is going right deep down into life and not caring a damn...' He was created a Knight of the British Empire in the New Year's Honours List in 1975. In a BBC interview he said that he had no ambition left now that he had been knighted and there was a waxwork of him in Madame Tussaud's. He died on St Valentine's Day in 1975 at the age of ninety-three.

P. G. WODEHOUSE

FRENCH LEAVE

PENGUIN BOOKS

PENGUIN BOOKS

Published by the Penguin Group
Penguin Books Ltd, 27 Wrights Lane, London W8 5TZ, England
Penguin Books USA Inc., 375 Hudson Street, New York, New York 10014, USA
Penguin Books Australia Ltd, Ringwood, Victoria, Australia
Penguin Books Canada Ltd, 10 Alcorn Avenue, Toronto, Ontario, Canada M4V 3B2
Penguin Books (NZ) Ltd, 182–190 Wairau Road, Auckland 10, New Zealand

Penguin Books Ltd, Registered Offices: Harmondsworth, Middlesex, England

First published by Herbert Jenkins Ltd 1956
This edition published by Barrie & Jenkins Ltd 1974
Published in Penguin Books 1992
5 7 9 10 8 6 4

Copyright 1956 by P. G. Wodehouse
Copyright © P. G. Wodehouse, 1974
All rights reserved

Printed in England by Clays Ltd, St Ives plc

Preface

French Leave puzzles me a bit. As a rule I can remember clearly how each of my books came to be written—how I got the central idea and so on—but this one baffles me. I wrote it in 1956 after I had been settled in Remsenburg for several years, and why in these American surroundings I suddenly decided that my next one was to have a French setting and a good many French characters is a mystery. The book ought to belong to the period 1930-1935, when I was living near Cannes and trying to learn French by going to the local Berlitz School and reading the novels of Colette, the plays of Georges Courteling and the sprightly contents of "La Vie Parisienne".

I never succeeded in speaking French, but I learned to read it all right, which is all I need, for now that I am 92 and never leave my Long Island home it is improbable that I shall have the opportunity of kidding back and forth with a Frenchman, and my views on pencils will remain unspoken.

Pencils, owing to my instructress at Berlitz, were the only subject on which I was able to speak with authority. She taught me all I know today about pencils (or crayons as we call them in France). 'Le crayon est jaune', I learned to say. 'Le crayon est bleu'. 'Donnez-moi le crayon de ma tante', and lots more on this fascinating topic. If some French manufacturer of pencils had happened along, I would have held him spellbound with my knowledge of his business, but in general society the difficulty of working pencils into the conversation was too much for me and after a while I gave it up and stuck to the normal grunts and gurgles of the foreigner who finds himself cornered by anything Gallic.

The thing I remember best about this book is that somebody gave it a nasty review in one of the weeklies, and Evelyn Waugh rushed to my defence and attacked the blighter with tooth and claw, starting a controversy which lasted for months. I have often wondered why this sort of thing is not done more often, for it brightens up whole issues of periodicals which badly need brightening up, besides giving the recipient of the stinker the comfortable feeling that he is not without friends and allies.

Was the fellow right? (Not Evelyn Waugh, the other fellow.) Very possibly. I am lucky in not being able to detect anything wrong with my stuff. I always think it is just like mother made. Others may not, but I do. When I have finished a novel and rewritten it and written it all again and polished up the spots that still want polishing, I get a sort of cosy glow and the feeling that it's all right. I have this feeling on re-reading *French Leave*. It seems to me that Nicolas Jules St Xavier Auguste, Marquis de Maufringneuse et Valerir-Moberanne is pretty good. I don't say he doesn't owe something to Georges Courteline, but even Shakespeare had his sources. He is not perhaps an admirable character, but we can't all be admirable characters, and he ends up well. I also like Mr Clutterbuck, the publisher, though he is much too fond of food.

A word on the title. I have not actually come across them, but I assume that everybody who has written a novel with a French setting must have called it what I have called mine. I wonder my American publisher did not change it. Changing titles is an occupational disease with American publishers. As A. A. Milne said when they altered the title of his Autobiography from *It's Too Late Now* to *What Luck*, 'This is a habit of American publishers. I fancy that the Order of Installation—taken (as I see it) in shirt sleeves, with blue pencil upheld in right hand, ends "And I do solemnly swear that whatsoever the author shall have called any novel submitted to me, and however suitable his title shall be, I will immediately alter it to one of my own choosing, thus asserting by a single stroke the dignity of my office and my own independence."

For some reason my *French Leave* got by and joined all the other French Leaves. I can only hope it will be found worthy to be included in the list of the Best Hundred Books Entitled *French Leave*.

P. G. Wodehouse

CHAPTER ONE

IF you search that portion of the state of New York known as Long Island with a sufficiently powerful magnifying glass, you will find, tucked away on the shore of the Great South Bay, the tiny village of Bensonburg. Its air is bracing, its scenery picturesque, its society mixed. You get all sorts there—the rich in their summer homes—men like Russell Clutterbuck, the publisher—and mingled with them the dregs or proletariat, the all-the-year-round-ers who have to scrape for a living. The Trent girls, daughters of the late Edgar Trent, the playwright, did their scraping in a small farm at the bottom of one of the lanes that led down to the water.

It is not likely that the name Edgar Trent will be familiar to many people today. He wrote only one real success, a farce called *Brother Masons*, and that was a long time ago. Still, *Brother Masons* brought in a good deal of money, and he was able on his death to leave some of it to his daughters Kate, Josephine and Teresa. They bought this Bensonburg farm—Kate's idea—and started to keep hens, with bees as a side line. Jo had wanted ducks, but was overruled by a majority vote. Hens, Terry said quite correctly, are no Chanel Number Five, but at least they stop short of smelling like an escape of sewer gas, which ducks in bulk do not, and Kate said that nobody in her senses would have made such a suggestion. Kate was several years older than the other two and always rather inclined to treat them as problem children.

On the afternoon of what was to be a momentous day for the house of Trent, Terry, having fed the hens and taken a wary look at the bees, came into the kitchen and found Jo there packing eggs in boxes, eyeing them morosely as she did so. She was a strikingly pretty girl, prettier even than Terry, whom any discriminating male would have thought quite pretty enough. She and Terry between them established a corner in the family good looks, taking after their mother. Kate was more like her father, whose forte had been intellect rather than beauty.

"Eggs!" said Jo disgustedly. "There ought to be a law."

Terry nodded sympathetically.

"I know what you mean. Here we are, young, ardent, idealistic, yearning for life and love and laughter, and what do we get? Eggs. How many have you broken so far?"

"Only two, both bad."

"Hetty's. She will go hiding them."

"And doesn't even cackle."

"I know. It's the deceit of the thing that hurts one. I hate these strong silent hens."

"I hate all hens. The mere mention of the word gives me a sinking feeling these days. Henry Weems wants me to call him Hen. He said he was always called that in the office. I told him it was the last straw."

"Was he asking you to marry him again?"

"Yes."

"Well, why don't you? You like him."

"Yes, I like him. I'm very fond of Henry. But what about my great scheme? Suppose that television sale goes through."

It was to the sale of *Brother Masons* that she referred. Someone with a retentive memory had remembered that ancient Broadway hit, and negotiations for what Henry

Weems, of the legal firm of Kelly, Dubinsky, Wix, Weems and Bassinger, who was handling the matter, called its transference to the television screen were proceeding. Jo was hopeful. Terry had been pessimistic from the start.

"It won't," she said. "Television sales never go through. The hellhounds of the system are all ghouls and sadists. It gives them a kick to dangle bags of gold before the eyes of the widow and the orphan and then shout 'April fool!' and snatch them away again. These facts are well known to students of the industry."

"Nothing doing, you think?"

"Nothing."

"I see. Well, thanks for cheering me up."

"Don't give it a thought. Just the Teresa Trent service. No, I'm afraid your great scheme is off, ducky. It was only a dream, anyway. You be a sensible girl and marry Henry. He . . . Hullo," said Terry, breaking off and walking to the window. "What goes on here? A car has stopped outside. Who can that be?"

"Probably Kate. She's out peddling honey. I suppose she thumbed a lift from someone."

"No, it's not Kate, it's a man. A man richly apparelled in a Palm Beach suit and . . . Why, blow me if it isn't Henry!"

"Henry!" Jo leaped up, setting eggs rolling dangerously in all directions. "Do you think this means something?"

"It looks like it. He surely hasn't driven eighty-five miles just to pass the time of day. Come, Watson, the hunt is up," said Terry, making for the door. "Let's go and see what it's all about."

Henry Weems had alighted from his car. He was a grave, solid young man, at the moment merely a minor unit of the firm which employed him but obviously destined some day to become a senior partner. At the sight of Jo a dull flush spread itself over his face and his nice eyes glowed. The sight of Jo always affected him powerfully.

"Oh—er—good afternoon," he said. "I am on my way to Easthampton, and I thought I would look in and tell you the news. Ouch!" said Henry, changing the subject, and explained that a bee had stung him.

This seemed to Jo a frivolous side-issue.

"Never mind the bee. What's the news?"

Terry frowned on what she considered a callous attitude toward one who was practically a stretcher case. She knew those bees. They bit like serpents and stung like adders.

"A little more womanly sympathy, my girl," she said. "The gentleman is at death's door. I'll get a blue bag."

"No, no, please, thank you. It doesn't matter."

"Those bees attack everyone except Kate. She cows them with the strength of her personality."

"What's the news?" said Jo. "What's the NEWS?"

Henry Weems had been hoping, lawyerlike, to spin the thing out quite a good deal before coming to the point, but seeing that quick action was desired, he leaped to what he would have called the *res*.

"It's all right about that television contract. The sale went through this morning."

"Oh, joy!" said Jo.

"Oh, bliss!" said Terry. "You've really swung it, have you?"

"I shall, of course, be writing you a formal letter, but I thought that as I was in the neighbourhood——"

"How much do we get?"

"Well, after deducting legal expenses——"

"Oh, gosh!" said Jo. "It isn't going to be like that Thing and Thing thing in *Bleak House*, is it, where all the money went to the lawyers?"

Henry gave her a reproachful look.

"I have kept the charges down to a minimum. Naturally I would do that for you ... and—er—of course, your sisters."

"I'm sure you would, Henry," said Terry heartily, "and we're terrifically grateful to you for all the trouble you've taken. You've been simply wonderful. I can see just what must have happened as clearly as if I had been there. Those fiends wanted to skin us and pay about thirty cents, and you stood up to them like some knight of old, and made them scare the moths out of their pocket-books."

"There was at the outset a certain discrepancy between what they offered and what I was prepared to accept on your behalf. This was subsequently adjusted."

"I can see you adjusting it! Did you thump the table?"

"I did once or twice."

"I'll bet you did. You've got character, Henry. That's what I like about you. You're solid and dependable. And what was the final score?"

It cost Henry a passing pang not to preface his statement with a few 'whereases' and 'co-heirs and assigns of Edgar Trent deceased, author of the dramatic composition entitled *Brother Masons*', but he made the sacrifice.

"You each get approximately two thousand dollars," he said. "And, of course, the eldest Miss Trent a similar sum."

Jo looked at Terry.

"Just about enough," she said, "adding your bit to my bit."

"The ideal amount," said Terry. "If it had been more, we might have been tempted to hoard it. No sense in hoarding four thousand dollars."

Henry's eyebrows shot up.

"Well, really!"

"You don't agree?"

"I should call four thousand dollars a very nice nest-egg."

"Nest-egg!" said Jo, wincing.

"Yes, don't use expressions like that," said Terry. "We're sensitive."

Henry apologized.

"What I meant was that, invested in Government bonds, it would bring in——"

"—a mere pittance. And pittances are no good to Jo and me. I don't know what Kate will do with her share of the loot, but we are going to put ours into something marvellous and exciting."

"Then it can't be safe."

"We aren't worrying about that."

Henry sighed. He had been through this sort of thing before with widowed clients. It sometimes seemed to him that every time Kelly, Dubinsky and Company got stuck with a half-witted relict, the cry went round the office, 'Let Weems attend to this.'

"You women! You're all the same. You read some wildcat prospectus and start counting your chickens——"

"Can't you possibly——" said Jo.

"—keep the conversation off fowls?" said Terry.

Henry apologized again. He said it had slipped out.

"Do please," he urged, "be reasonable. Reserve at least half the money for sound securities. Don't put all your eggs into one . . . Oh, I beg your pardon. These proverbial expressions! Odd that so many of them should be associated with the poultry-farming industry. No doubt it dates back to a time when——"

He broke off and leaped a few inches skywards. A voice had spoken behind him. "Good afternoon, Mr. Weems," it said, and, turning, he perceived the formidable figure of his loved one's sister Kate, who always scared the daylights out of him. She reminded him of a governess of his childhood whose forceful personality had made a deep impression on his plastic mind.

"What a day I've had!" said Kate, hoarse with self-pity.

"Bad?" said Terry sympathetically.

"Nothing but grumbling and complaints. Mr. Clutter-buck was going on again about our charging too much for the honey."

"I keep telling him he's got to take into account the wear and tear on the bees. He can't expect bees to work for nothing. You pinned his ears back, I trust?"

"I was firm with him," said Kate, and Henry could well believe it. "But it was all very depressing."

"Well, here's something to cheer you up, old lady. Henry has put the *Brother Masons* deal through. You and Jo and I each get two thousand dollars. How's that for a tonic?"

Kate beamed. She ceased to droop.

"Excellent!" she said graciously, like Henry's governess when Henry had got a sum right. "This certainly is good news. Two thousand dollars! Really!"

"Henry was terrific. He intimidated the sons of Belial. He twisted their arms and rubbed his knuckles in their hair. They were as corn before his sickle."

"I'm sure they were," said Kate, more graciously than ever. "Will you have a glass of milk, Mr. Weems?"

"No, thank you."

"Of course you will. A glass of milk for Mr. Weems, Josephine."

"Coming right up."

"No, please, no milk."

"Have an egg," suggested Terry. "Said to be very strengthening."

"No, thank you, really. I must be getting along."

"I'll go and tell Jo. Good-bye, Henry, and thanks again ever so much. You've been wonderful. Milk's off," said Terry, joining Jo in the kitchen. "And Henry's off, too," she went on, as the chugging of a car blended with the cackling of hens. "I thought he wouldn't linger. Kate scares him stiff."

"She scares me most of the time."

"Me, too. We've both got the younger sister complex. You can't ever really lose your awe of someone who used to scrub your face with a soapy flannel. Are you looking forward to telling her about our plans?"

"No, I'm not."

"You haven't changed your mind about that?"

"Of course not. You aren't weakening, are you?"

"Not a bit. All right, I'll do the telling."

"Oh, Terry! Would you? I wonder what she'll say."

"We shall soon know, for here she comes. You'd better vanish."

Jo did so through the back door, and had scarcely left when Kate appeared.

A glance at Kate was enough to reveal that she was in no sportive mood. She began speaking before she had crossed the threshold.

"What," she demanded, "is all this I hear from Mr. Weems? He tells me you girls are talking of putting your share of this money into some risky venture where you'll lose every penny of it. Are you crazy?"

Terry braced herself for battle. It was not going to be easy, but then she had never anticipated that it would be.

"Crazy? I wonder. Perhaps we are. I'm afraid this is going to be a shock to you, Kate. Jo and I are going to use our money having a holiday."

"A holiday?"

"In France. We both speak French fairly well. Jo wants to go to St. Rocque on the Brittany coast. She was reading about it in a magazine. Apparently they have some sort of Festival there at the end of July, and there are big doings, she says. I prefer Roville in Picardy. I've always dreamed of going to Roville. It sounds wonderful. And now we've got these pennies from heaven——"

Kate had an illusion that the kitchen floor was heaving beneath her like a stage sea.

"Do you mean," she gasped, "that you propose to *squander* this money?"

"As far as I am concerned, yes. Every cent of it. I want one lovely big splash which I'll remember all my life, and then I'll come back to the hens and bees. Jo's idea is a bit more elaborate. She's hoping to marry a millionaire."

"What!"

"Lots of them in those parts."

"Do you mean that she is deliberately going to try to marry for money?"

"I wouldn't put it like that. She's just going where money is. It's perfectly logical, really. Nine times out of ten you marry in your own set. Go around with plumbers, and you'll end by marrying a plumber. Mix with millionaires, and you're quite likely to marry a millionaire. That seems to be the way she's worked it out. She's going to France to give the millionaires a chance at her, and I'm going with her to keep her company."

"I forbid you to do this insane thing!"

"I'm sorry. I knew you wouldn't like it. But it's all settled."

Kate sank into a chair, and was silent for a moment.

"What are you going to do for clothes?" she asked.

"We shall buy them in Paris."

Kate sniffed.

"If you're going to buy a lot of expensive clothes and stay at expensive hotels and lead the sort of life they lead at those places, your money won't last long."

"No, we realized that. Here's how we have planned it out. We shall take it in turns to be the rich Miss Trent. We draw cards, and the winner has first go. She has a

month of wealth and excitement, the loser acting as her
maid. A girl travelling alone has to have a maid. At the
end of the month the loser takes over and has her month
—somewhere else, naturally—with the former winner
acting as *her* maid . . . and so on as long as the money holds
out. Rotating crops," said Terry.

Kate's face was drawn and set.

"Are you really resolved to do this?"

"Yes, absolutely and definitely."

"Then I shall come with you."

"Why, Kate, that's wonderful. We'll pay your
expenses, of course. This is our treat. We'll have a
marvellous time. You'll love St. Rocque and revel in
Roville."

"I expect to loathe both of them. But I am not going to
have you two children wandering all over Europe alone,"
said Kate, and strode out.

Jo peeped in at the back door.

"How did it go?" she asked.

"Better than I expected. She's coming with us."

"Oh, gosh!"

"My good child, it's the best thing that could have happened. I don't say Kate is the ideal companion for a mad
jaunt in the world's pleasure centres, but she'll be a
chaperone, and you would have got nowhere without a
chaperone. Your aim is to excite interest, and the girl
who excites interest is the girl with a chaperone, a personal
maid and a faint air of mystery. Now we can proceed.
Where are the cards? Here we are. Let's go. Which of
us is to be the rich Miss Trent and which Fellowes, the
lowly maid? I like the name Fellowes, don't you? I
found it in an English novel. You draw first."

Jo drew.

"Five."

"I can beat that on my head. I shall now proceed to

draw a king or a queen or a . . . *Three!* Oh, death and damnation!"

"Fellowes," said Jo, "you strangely forget yourself, my good girl."

Darkness had fallen on Bensonburg, the velvet darkness of summer night. Hens, which had cackled since early morning, sat mute on their roosts and the last bee, finding nobody left to sting, had winged its way back to the hive. The new moon hung in the sky like a silver sickle, and Terry, as she stood in the little garden outside the kitchen door, bowed to it three times. She found herself a little breathless. She was wondering what the future had in store for her.

Among the things which the future had in store for her were that exuberant old gentleman, the Marquis de Maufringneuse, his son the Comte d'Escrignon, Mrs. Winthrop Pegler of Park Avenue and Newport, Frederick ('Butch') Carpenter, majority stockholder in the well-known sparkling table-water, Fizzo, J. Russell Clutterbuck of the publishing house of Winch and Clutterbuck, and last but not least—the *bonne-bouche*, as it were—Pierre Alexandre Boissonade, Commissaire of Police.

CHAPTER TWO

AS the clocks of Paris were striking eleven on a morning three weeks after the Bensonburg expeditionary force had set out for Europe, a tall, willowy, elegant figure, dressed in the extreme of fashion, turned the corner of the Rue Belleau and entered the Rue Vanaye. It was Nicolas Jules St Xavier Auguste, Marquis de Maufringneuse et Valerie-Moberanne, affectionately known to his friends, of whom he had many in all walks of life, as Old Nick. He was on his way to the Ministry de Dons et Legs (which is pronounced 'lay' and means legacies), where he occupied the position of *employé attaché à l'expédition du troisième bureau* (which means clerk). He walked hurriedly, for a summer storm was raging over the city and he had no umbrella. There was a cloud on his handsome face. The thought of having to work always depressed him.

Until a few years previously, when his rich American wife had divorced him, work and he had been strangers. He had, so to speak, dwelt in marble halls with vassals and serfs at his side. But that was all over now. His only assets in the world today, apart from a meagre monthly salary, were his distinguished looks, his unconquerable spirit and the superb assortment of suits, boots, ties, shirts, socks and underwear, mostly unpaid for, to which he clung firmly through his worst vicissitudes.

It was some twenty minutes after he had entered the gloomy cubbyhole which he shared with his colleagues M. Soupe and M. Letondu that in a larger, airier office down the corridor M. de La Hourmerie, the department's director, stretched out a hand and pressed the bell on his desk.

An underling appeared.

"The dossier Quibolle, Ovide," said M. de La Hourmerie.

"Very good, monsieur."

"I think M. Soupe has it."

"No, monsieur. M. le Marquis de Maufringneuse. He was working on it when I went in a moment ago."

M. de La Hourmerie started. He seemed stunned.

"The Marquis?"

"Yes, monsieur."

"You mean he is here?"

"Yes, monsieur."

"Here in the office?"

"Yes, monsieur."

A stern look came into M. de La Hourmerie's face, the look of a man who suspects that he is being trifled with.

"Be careful, Ovide. Think before you speak. Weigh your words. Do you seriously assert that the Marquis de Maufringneuse, clerk of the third bureau, is at his post . . . *working?*"

"Yes, monsieur."

"Incredible!" M. de La Hourmerie recovered himself with a visible effort. "Send him to me," he said, "and tell him to bring the dossier Quibolle with him."

The summons found Old Nick staring moodily at the document in question, to which he had long taken a vivid dislike. It was something to do with the gift to the Ministry of a museum or something of that sort by the Mayor and citizens of some rural community, and he had never been able to make head or tail of it. Thrusting it into his pocket, he went down the corridor with the air of a good man persecuted. He had a soul above these petty things.

But his dark moods never lasted long, and by the time he arrived at the director's sanctum his geniality had returned and he was smiling his charming smile—or, as it seemed to M. de La Hourmerie, grinning like an ape. In the rank undergrowth of M. de La Hourmerie's prejudices there was no more luxuriant weed than his abhorrence of Old Nick's charming smile.

"Good morning, monsieur."

"Good morning, M. le Marquis."

"Still raining," said Old Nick affably, glancing at the window. "And of course I came out without my umbrella. One always does, does one not? Did I ever tell you, by the way, about my idea for an Umbrella Club?"

"Never mind about your Umbrella Club."

Old Nick abandoned a subject which had obviously failed to grip, and became brisk and business-like.

"You wished to see me?" he said.

"I wished," replied M. de La Hourmerie acidly, forgetting all about the dossier Quibolle in the artistic thrill of finding the neat retort, "but I never hoped to. Your being here is such a phenomenon, such an anomaly. It is, I think, two weeks since you last visited the Ministry."

Old Nick blessed his soul.

"Not really?"

"I assure you."

"As long as that? How the days slip by!"

"They do indeed. Stop grinning, M. le Marquis."

"I was smiling."

"Stop smiling," said M. de La Hourmerie.

There was a pause, during which—uninvited—Old Nick took a chair.

"This being so," said M. de La Hourmerie, resuming, "you will perhaps not consider me unduly impetuous when I request an explanation. The Civil Service of France has its traditions, and one of them is that the *personnel* shall perform their duties with a certain languor. We expect it. In a way we like it. In a vulgar rushing age it lends, as it were, a touch of the picturesque, a suggestion of old-world dignity. But there are limits. Two weeks, M. le Marquis! Two weeks during which you have not set foot in the Administration. Would it be incommoding you if I asked you to give me your reasons for this abstention? And don't," he went on quickly, "tell me that you have been attending the funerals of a series of your aunts."

"I have no aunts."

"Nephews?"

"No nephews. I have a son called Jefferson, of all absurd names," said Old Nick chattily. "My wife—my first wife—dead these many years, poor soul—insisted on calling him that. She was American. So, oddly enough, was my second wife, from whom I was parted in the divorce court. My son Jefferson is a writer. He writes stories and things."

He spoke disapprovingly. The son and heir of a Marquis de Maufringneuse, he considered, ought not to be frittering away his youth scribbling, he should be out and about looking for a rich wife in the fine old Maufringneuse family tradition. Anyone as attractive as his son Jefferson, felt Old Nick, ought by this time to have been comfortably attached to the pay-roll of the daughter of a millionaire, if he had had the right stuff in him.

M. de La Hourmerie was not interested in the young man's literary efforts, only in his physical fitness.

"He is in good health, this son of yours?"

"Oh, excellent. He roughed it in America for some years, and he was in the Maquis in the late war. That toughened him."

"I am relieved. For I will not conceal it from you that I find myself regarding with a jaundiced eye the growing mortality among the relatives of members of my staff.

'My excuses, M. le Directeur, that I must absent myself
from my duties, I have lost a cousin.' 'My excuses, M. le
Directeur, that I am unable to appear at the bureau. I
have lost an uncle.' Every day! They die off like flies,
these cousins, aunts and uncles. It is a massacre, a veri-
table massacre. Attila the Hun never created havoc on
such a scale."

Old Nick tut-tutted sympathetically. He could quite
see how the other must find this sort of thing annoying.
He leaned back in his chair, trying to think what animal it
was that M. de La Hourmerie reminded him of. He
decided that he looked like a pug dog.

"So, as I say," continued the director, "I am rejoiced
that M. le Comte is for the moment robust. We seek, then,
elsewhere for your reasons for depriving us of your society.
Here, in a word, is the position. The third bureau con-
sists of yourself, M. Soupe and M. Letondu. M. Soupe is in
his forty-second year of service, and one cannot reasonably
expect from him more than a senile goodwill. M. Letondu,
though in the prime of life, has for some weeks shown every
sign of being off his head."

"Mad as a hatter," agreed Old Nick, "and seems to
have taken a particular dislike to you, for some reason.
He says he's going to murder you with a hatchet he bought
the other day."

"Indeed?" said M. de La Hourmerie indifferently, as
if feeling that this would be perfectly in order provided that
it were done out of office hours. "But if you will permit me
to continue what I was saying. We have then, to carry on
the work of the third bureau, two officials of subnormal in-
telligence and yourself, and you are never there. It is a
state of things that cannot be permitted to go on, so I ask
you to be frank with me, M. le Marquis. Why do you
abstain from your duties in this manner?"

Old Nick reflected.

"I attribute it largely to the weather."

"I beg your pardon?"

"It has been so extraordinarily fine till today. The beaming sun. The blue skies. The fleecy clouds. The soft breezes. Ah, Paris in the springtime!"

"It is not springtime. It is the middle of July."

"Ah, Paris in the middle of July!" said Old Nick, amiably accepting the correction. "Take a typical morning like yesterday."

"Or fifty other yesterdays."

"What happens? I wake. I rise. I shave. I bathe. I breakfast. I take my hat and cane. I say to myself 'And now for the bureau'. I go out into the street, and at once I am in a world of sunshine and laughter and happiness, a world in which it seems ridiculous to be shut up in a stuffy office with the senile Soupe and the homicidal Letondu. And all of a sudden . . . how it happens I couldn't tell you . . . I find myself in a chair on the boulevard, a cigarette between my lips, coffee and a cognac in front of me. It's a most mysterious state of affairs."

"A state of affairs which cannot——"

"But I am strong," proceeded Old Nick. "I take out my watch and lay it on the table. 'When the hands point to eleven,' I say to myself, 'Ho for the bureau.' And when they point to eleven, I say 'Ho for the bureau when they point to half past'. And when they point to half past——"

"You wait till noon and then go off to lunch?"

"Exactly."

"And after lunch the same thing happens?"

"Precisely. It goes on day after day. It's most distressing. I fret. I lose weight."

"Then might I ask what has brought you here this morning?"

"It was raining," said Old Nick simply.

"I see." M. de La Hourmerie's voice was grim. He pushed himself slowly up from his chair, and Old Nick uttered a protesting cry.

"My dear sir, don't do that! Don't ever do that."

"I beg your pardon?"

"Push yourself out of a chair in that middle-aged way. We are none of us getting younger, of course, but we can school ourselves to hold the advancing years in check. You should rise like this," said Old Nick, executing a nimble leap. "Tell me, my dear fellow," he said, re-seating himself, "are you a leg lifter? When you wish to place one leg over the other, do you use your hands? Thus, as if you were hoisting a sack of coals? Correct this habit. Don't do it, my good sir. I could supply you with a whole list of don'ts. As for instance, don't shuffle. Walk with a springy step. Don't rub your knee after kneeling or your chest after going upstairs. Don't neglect your before-breakfast deep-breathing exercises. Don't cough. Don't make a noise when drinking soup. Don't snore. If you do, use two pillows or in extreme cases three. And always remember," said Old Nick, wagging a monitory finger, "that the greyer the hair, the more important the barber, and the less youthful the figure, the more fastidious must be the clothes."

It was possibly the finger that caused M. de La Hourmerie at this moment to lose his dignified calm. A man of his position resents the wagging fingers of subordinates. For perhaps a minute he spoke fluently and well, and when he was obliged to suspend his remarks in order to refill his lungs—a system of deep-breathing exercises before break-fast would, of course, have rendered this unnecessary—he saw that his efforts had not been wasted. Old Nick was staring at him incredulously.

"But this—correct me if I am wrong—this sounds as if you were dismissing me," he said.

"I am," M. de La Hourmerie assured him. "I am aware that in the Civil Service it is more customary to request a resignation, but there are times when a mere resignation will not suffice."

"Reflect!"

"I have reflected."

"Reflect again. I think you're making a serious mistake. I mean ... Well, one doesn't want to talk about one's ancient lineage and all that, but have you considered that the presence in it of a Marquis de Maufringneuse sheds—shall we say a lustre—on the Ministry de Dons Et Legs? Gives it a tone, as it were?"

"It is precisely the presence of the Marquis de Maufringneuse that I have been anxious to obtain. All I have had to date is his absence."

Old Nick digested this.

"That's rather good," he said, always ready to give praise where praise was due.

"Thank you," said de La Hourmerie, who thought so, too. "That, then, is all, M. Le Marquis. Good morning."

Old Nick rose. He was a resilient man, and any slight dismay he may have felt had passed.

"Ah, well," he said, looking, as was always his habit, on the bright side. "It's the best time of the year for taking a little holiday, and it never does to keep the nose uninterruptedly to the grindstone. If the machine is not to break down, it needs constant periods of rest and repose. Any doctor will tell you that. I think I'll go to Biarritz."

"You may go to the devil."

"No, not Biarritz. St. Rocque. The Festival, you know. I was forgetting the Festival. One meets all the best people at St. Rocque during Festival Week. Then I will be saying good-bye. Good-bye for the moment, of course, for I feel sure that on giving the matter thought you will reconsider this mad decision of yours to dispense with

my services. I'll let you have my address and generally
keep in touch from time to time. Oh, by the way," said
Old Nick, "there is just one thing. I happen at the
moment to be a little short of cash. Could you possibly . . . ?
No? Quite all right, my dear fellow, quite all right. No
doubt you have many calls on your purse. I will go and
see what my son Jefferson can do about it."

Having returned to the office and bidden farewell to M.
Soupe, who gaped at him with what M. de La Hourmerie
had described as senile goodwill, and M. Letondu, who
took no notice of him, seeming to be brooding on hatchets,
Old Nick placed hat on head at a jaunty angle and left the
building, twirling his cane. The rain had stopped, and
sunshine was flooding the streets. He walked to his rooms
and, reaching them, became aware of some bulky substance
in his pocket. It was the dossier Quibolle. Whistling a
gay air, he threw it into the drawer where he kept his handkerchiefs, adjusted his hat again and set out for the Rue
Jacob, where Jefferson, Comte d'Escrignon, maintained a
modest bed-sitting-room.

CHAPTER THREE

IT was only in the last year or two that Old Nick had seen much of his son and heir, for almost immediately after his father's second marriage the young man, disliking his stepmother—and Old Nick did not blame him—had removed himself from the family circle and gone to America, where he had supported himself in a fashion till the outbreak of the war. He now lived in Paris and spent his time writing, as Old Nick had said, stories and things, with such limited success that Old Nick felt himself justified in mourning over him as a prodigal son. Good looks, easy manners, the Maufringneuse charm . . . the boy had them all, and apparently no intention of ever cashing in on them. It was, in Old Nick's opinion, bitter. The young fellow had not yet brought his father's grey hairs in sorrow to the grave, but he felt that it was the sort of thing that might happen at any time.

Arriving at this disappointing young man's lodgings, he found him in his shirt-sleeves, hammering away at a typewriter almost as ancient as the lineage of the Maufringneuses.

"Hullo, Nick," he said, turning and perceiving the author of his being. "Take a seat. Better dust it first. And don't let me hear a word out of you for at least ten minutes. I'm working."

Jefferson, Comte d'Escrignon, was the fruit of Old Nick's first marriage, to Loretta Ann, only daughter of Jefferson Potter and his wife Emily of Ridgfield, Connecticut, in the United States of America. This was in the 'twenties, when the flower of American youth was migrating to Paris in a manner reminiscent of the great race movements of the Middle Ages and all young men and women with souls and even the remotest ability to handle pen or paint brush went flocking to answer the call of the *rive gauche*.

Loretta Ann, who painted, was allowed by her parents to join the mob, and she was painting one morning in the Luxembourg Gardens when Old Nick, then a very young Nick, came along. In Bohemian fashion they got into conversation and three weeks later, Old Nick's views on rich marriages being different in those days, became man and wife. In due season their union was blessed, and Old Nick, already weakened by the sight of the revolting poached-egg-like little object tucked under his bride's right arm, was further shattered by the news that he was going to have to call it Jefferson.

However, Time the great healer had done its work. The child had picked up in looks as the years went by, and Old Nick had become, if not reconciled, at least resigned to his name. So when his son, ceasing to hammer the keys, leaned back and seemed ready for conversation, it was with only the slightest sensation of nausea that he said:

"Well, Jafe, my boy. You seem busy, Jafe."

"I have to finish this thing by tomorrow."

"Then I mustn't interrupt you."

"That's all right. I'm well ahead."

"How are you doing these days?"

"Oh, I get along. I make enough to live on and hope the dawn will come."

"Dawn? I don't understand you."

"A poetic way of saying I am hoping to sell my novel."

"Is this your novel?"

"Good heavens, no. This is just a hack job. A *feuilleton* for one of the evening papers. The novel's over in America. I sent it to a publisher called Clutterbuck."

"Clutterbuck?" Old Nick considered the name. "Ah, well, why not Clutterbuck?" he said, for he was a broad-minded man. "Some Americans are called Quacken-bush. Your stepmother married one of them after she divorced me. You met this Clutterbuck when you were in America?"

"No, we aren't acquainted. A friend of mine on the Paris *New York Herald-Tribune* knows him and gave me a letter to him. That was a couple of months ago, and dead silence ever since. I suppose Clutterbuck is learning to read. But how do you happen to be in these parts at this time of day, Nick? Aren't you working at the Ministry?"

"No longer. I ought never to have accepted employ-ment at such a place. It was a mistake."

"Did your boss think that, too?"

"Certainly not. He was in despair when I tendered my resignation. But I stuck to my guns."

"And what are you going to do now?"

"I thought of taking a little holiday at St. Rocque. My friend Prince Blamont-Chevry is there. And that brings me to the reason of my visit, Jafe."

A quick smile, charming like his father's, lit up Jeff's face. He was a striking-looking young man, tall and dark and wiry with a humorous mouth and quick brown eyes and the strong chin which he had inherited from his mother's side of the family. The Potters had all had strong chins. Those of the Maufringneuses tended to recede a little.

"How much?" he asked.

"Could you manage ten thousand francs?"

"You wouldn't settle for five?"

"Ten would be better."

"All right. Here you are."

"Thank you, Jafe. This will be a great help. By the way, do you know any men with money?"

"Only you. Why?"

"I was thinking of my Umbrella Club."

"What's that?"

"Haven't I ever mentioned it to you? It's an idea I got from a delightful book of reminiscences by a couple of musical comedy writers. It is based, as all great schemes are, on human nature. It is human nature to want to keep dry when it rains, but it is also human nature not to want to carry about a great clumsy umbrella all the time. My Club solves this problem. You enrol yourself as a member. You pay an entrance fee and dues. This entitles you to wear a badge. You are caught in the rain. You step into the nearest tobacconist's or kiosk, show your badge and receive an umbrella, for which you are charged some nominal sum. When the rain stops, you step into another tobacconist's and deposit the umbrella. Simple, but I see a vast fortune in it. A million members——"

"How are you going to get your million members?"

"Ah! That is the difficulty, of course. One would need capital to start such an enterprise. If only you would marry, Jafe!"

Jeff sighed. He had been wondering when this subject would come up.

"It is my dearest wish to see you married. Provided, of course, that the settlements are right."

"Would you have me sell myself for gold?"

"Certainly, and the more gold the better."

"Aren't you a little short of soul, Nick?"

"What do you mean? I have plenty of soul, more than I know what to do with."

"I wouldn't call you romantic."

Old Nick dismissed romance with a wave of the hand.

"In this hard post-war world, my boy, there is no room for moonlit sentiment. The head must rule the heart."

"You didn't always feel that way, did you?"

"You mean when I married your mother? I was young and foolish then."

"Well, I'm young and foolish now."

A look of alarm shot into Old Nick's face.

"Don't tell me you've been mad enough to go and get yourself involved with some frightful female pauper?"

"Oh, no. I'm not young and foolish in any special direction. Just young and foolish."

Old Nick puffed out a relieved breath.

"I thought for a moment . . . You frightened me, my boy. You're a writer, and one never knows what a writer is going to do next. And you're just at the age when you might have had a girl's name tattooed on your chest, which is always the first step to disaster. I attribute my whole success in life to a rigid observance of the fundamental rule—Never have yourself tattooed with any woman's name, not even her initials. But to return to what we were talking about, I cannot understand this reluctance of yours to make a rich marriage. It must be the Potter strain in you coming out. Sturdy middle-class Americans like the Potters do have this odd prejudice against the marriage of convenience. I can't see it myself. One contracting party supplies the blue blood, the other the money. Perfectly normal business arrangement, it seems to me. Still, it's no good arguing with you, I suppose. You're as obstinate as a mule. Your mother was the same. Would insist on having you called Jefferson. No moving her. I remember once, when I was trying to reason with her on the point, she got a bucket of water and poured it all over me. The room was like a lake. I can still see the cat flying from the flood with its tail about a yard long. Did you know that when a cat's tail gets wet, it lengthens? It does," said Old Nick, and on this nature note took his departure.

Jeff resumed work on his *feuilleton*.

CHAPTER FOUR

IN stating that there were big doings at the Brittany resort of St. Rocque at the end of July Jo had been quite correct. Normally staid and peaceful, the town comes then to sudden life, with everybody—residents and summer visitors alike—pulling together in a body and giving of their best. Who St. Rocque was and what he did to win canonization few probably of the former and certainly none of the latter have the slightest idea, but that does not prevent them celebrating his Festival with a whole-hearted gusto which for twenty-four hours makes the place a perfect hell.

Or so thought Kate as she sat with Terry in Jo's suite at the Hotel Magnifique.

"Oh, for goodness' sake shut that window!" she said, as a brass band, giving the impression of being in the room, burst abruptly into a popular march.

"We shall stifle," Terry pointed out.

"I'd rather stifle than be deafened. It's been pandemonium all day. I put my head out of the hotel for an instant this morning and a man dressed as a Corsican bandit blew a squeaker in my face."

"Probably somebody shy nervously trying to break the ice. I do wish you were enjoying all this more."

"Enjoying!"

"It makes me feel so guilty and remorseful having dragged you out here."

"Too late to think of that now."

Terry sighed. This was one of Kate's difficult evenings.

The Festival of the Saint had brought to the surface all that was most austere in her.

"Perhaps you will like Roville better," she suggested hopefully.

"It will probably be worse than this."

"It's bound to be quieter, anyway. Listen to that noise. I'd love to go and see what's going on."

"Well, you are not to. Goodness knows what might happen to you. The whole place seems to have gone crazy. I don't like the idea of Josephine being out on a night like this."

"Oh, Jo's all right. She's dining with Chester Todd."

"So she told me. Who is this man Todd?"

"You've met him. Jo brought him in for drinks one afternoon."

"I wasn't there."

"That's right. Nor you were. He's a friend of the Mr. Carpenter who owns that enormous yacht that's in the harbour. They came from Cannes."

"But what sort of a man is he?"

"Young, amiable, rich. Not much brains, from the little I was able to gather while serving the cocktails, but Jo likes him. I hope she pulls if off."

Kate snorted.

"'Pulls it off!' What an expression. Deliberately hunting a husband. I think it's disgraceful."

As she spoke, Jo came in, looking so spectacular that Terry uttered a squeal of admiration.

"Joseph-ine! That dress!"

"Is it all right?"

"It's out of this world. I can hardly wait till I'm wearing it."

"That'll be next week, worse luck. Do you like it, Kate?"

"I am going to bed," said Kate coldly. "I don't suppose I shall get a wink of sleep with all this hideous din, but one may be able to bear it better lying down."

"Kate's in a dangerous mood," said Terry, as the door closed. "She doesn't approve of you going out with Chester Todd tonight."

"I've got to go out with Chester Todd tonight, and any other night he asks me. I can't waste a minute. My month's up next Tuesday."

"I'll lend you two weeks of my month, if you like."

"Will you?" Jo's face lit up. "Oh, Terry, you are an angel. Another two weeks might just about do it."

"'Do it!' What an expression. Deliberately hunting a husband. I think it's disgraceful."

"Did Kate say that?"

"Verbatim."

"Kate's a bohunkus. Doesn't she realize that, if you want to marry the Fairy Prince, you can't sit at home waiting for him to come riding up on a white horse? You've got to go out and get him."

"It's a way of looking at it, I suppose. I don't feel like that myself, but if you do, go to it. How are things coming along?"

"I'm making progress."

"How about the Parker girl?"

Jo considered the point.

"Jane Parker. I know what you mean. She's always around, of course, but I don't believe she's a menace. They're more like brother and sister. I don't know how to describe it, but . . . Oh, you know. Nothing romantic."

"Will she be there tonight?"

"No, we're dining alone, and I ought to be going. You're sure the dress looks all right?"

"It'll knock his eye out."

"And you're sure you don't mind lending me those two weeks?"

"Of course not."

"You're wonderful. Are you going out?"

"No, I'm confined to barracks. I shall go and have a chat with Armand."

"Who's Armand?"

"The floor waiter. Great friend of mine."

"Oh, him? Sooner you than me. Well, good night, Fellowes, me girl. See you in the morning."

"Very good, moddom," said Terry, and went in to see how Kate was getting on.

Kate was gloomier than ever. Listening to the din of the Festival, she mourned and would not be comforted, and so depressing did Terry find her society that after half an hour of it she left her and went out into the corridor to talk to her friend Armand, whose conversation was always calculated to amuse, instruct and entertain.

Armand, himself reluctantly on duty, seemed surprised to find her still on the premises. He had supposed, he said, that she would have been out mingling with the gay throng.

"There is dancing—all night there is dancing—in the Public Amusement Gardens," said Armand.

An eager light came into Terry's eyes. Her feet began to move, and she sang softly a snatch of an old song.

"'Oh, Buffalo gals, won't you come out tonight, come out tonight, come out tonight and dance by the light of the moon?'"

"Pardon?" said Armand.

"It's all right, my old cabbage. I'm not arguing, just singing. But I've nobody to dance with."

Armand made light of this. Terry, he said, had only to present herself in the Public Amusement Gardens and a hundred partners would leap to minister to her pleasure. On the night of the Festival of the Saint, it appeared, St. Rocque forgot its Emily Post and dispensed with formal introductions. He strongly advised her to take advantage of an opportunity which might not occur again.

Terry chewed her lip thoughtfully.

"It's an idea. After all, one's only young once, isn't one?"

That, Armand agreed, was it in a nutshell.

"The trouble is, my movements are restricted. There is one who watches me like a hawk, spying out all my ways. Still, she may be asleep by now."

She went back into the suite and listened at Kate's door. Heavy breathing came from behind it. Despite the uproar of the Festival, Nature had taken toll of the tired frame.

She went into Jo's room. There was a dress in the closet there which she had been wanting to wear for weeks.

2

At about the same moment, lying on the bed in his bedroom at the dingy *pension* down by the harbour which was all his modest means had been able to afford, Old Nick sat up quickly—M. de La Hourmerie would have had to use his hands—and gazed expectantly at the door. Footsteps had paused outside it, the footsteps, he hoped, of his son Jefferson, whose coming he was so eagerly awaiting.

A bedraggled maid-of-all-work entered, in her hand a telegram. She gave it to him, sniffed and departed, and he tore it open, fearing the worst. It must, he thought, be from Jeff, regretting his inability to answer a father's cry for help.

It was not from Jeff. It read:

Where is the dossier Quibolle?

and was signed De La Hourmerie. Old Nick threw it from him with an impatient flick of the wrist. He had far too much on his mind to be able to give a thought to dossiers Quibolle. The dossier Quibolle was the least of his worries.

A quarter of an hour later, as he lay there in the depths,

the door opened again and Jeff appeared, just as he had given him up.

Jeff was looking dusty, weary and travel-stained. It is a long journey from Paris to St. Rocque, and the day had been warm. He sank into a rickety chair, gazed at his parent in a puzzled sort of way, as if wondering what he had done to deserve such an affliction, and closed his eyes. He was devoted to Old Nick, but there were moments when he found filial love waning.

Old Nick clicked his tongue.

"Don't go to sleep, Jafe."

"I'm awake . . . just. So you're in trouble again, Nick?"

"Grave trouble, my boy. You will have gathered that from my telegram. I expected you before this. I had supposed," said Old Nick reproachfully, "that you would have come flying on the wings of the wind."

"The best I could do was to come flying on the slowest train in France."

"You had a tiring journey?"

"Quite fatiguing."

"I'm sorry. Still, the great thing is that you are here. Jafe, my boy, I fear I shall have to bother you again. Could you possibly let me have fifteen thousand francs?"

"Oh, my God!"

"I know, I know," said Old Nick sympathetically. "I know just how you feel." A horrid thought struck him. "Haven't you got it?"

"I've got it—yes. They paid me for that *feuilleton*."

"Good!" said Old Nick, forgetting his prejudice against the life literary.

"Was that why you wired me to come here?"

"It was. Though I am always glad to see you, my boy, always."

"Couldn't you have written and saved me a long, dull, grubby train journey?"

Old Nick shook his head.

"Had I done so, there was the danger that you might not have let me have the money. It is so fatally easy to refuse by letter. One has to think of these things."

"How true. Well, here you are. But it's my heart's blood."

"I can well imagine it," said Old Nick courteously. "These are trying times for all of us. You probably noticed that in my telegram I said it was a matter of life and death. A figure of speech, of course, but not far from the truth. Had I failed to obtain the money by noon tomorrow, I should have gone to prison. To prison, my boy, and one shudders to think what the prisons must be like in these provincial resorts. They are bad enough, Prince Blamont-Chevry tells me, in Paris."

Jeff stared. His parent rarely had the power to surprise him, but he had done so now.

"Prison? Good heavens, Nick, what on earth have you been doing now?"

"I can understand your emotion," said Old Nick. "It is the old, old story. When a man's means become straitened, he is for ever tiptoeing between the lines of the law, and they keep printing them finer and finer all the time. Last night, alas, I bumped into one of them. Not my fault, I hasten to assure you. I was the innocent victim of circumstances. The whole disaster was brought about by the dastardly duplicity of Prince—a fine sort of Prince, upon my word—Blamont-Chevry."

"What did his highness do?"

Old Nick's voice quivered with pardonable indignation.

"He invited me to dinner. Nothing in writing, of course, but a clearly understood gentleman's agreement that he was to be the host. We went to what I suppose is the

best hotel in the town—certainly it was expensive enough—
and he entertained me lavishly, pressing food and wine
upon me regardless of cost.   At the conclusion of the meal,
which I will admit I enjoyed, for it was excellent, he
excused himself to go and make a telephone call. That was
the last I saw of him."

"He left you to pay the bill?   You do have some extraordinary friends, Nick."

"Blamont-Chevry is no longer a friend of mine.   I am a
tolerant man.   I can forgive much, but I cannot forgive his
behaviour of last night.   I would like to horsewhip him on
the steps of his club."

"But I suppose he hasn't a club?"

"No. That, of course, is the difficulty.   He had six at
one time, but has been expelled from all of them.   So there
I was, Jafe, with a hundred francs in my pocket——"

"What became of that ten thousand?"

"I had reverses at the Casino.   It's a long story.
No need to go into it now.   Well, there, as I say, I was
with a hundred francs in my pocket, faced—it was on
a plate on the table before me—with a bill for twelve
thousand."

"I thought you said fifteen."

"Of course, of course.   My mind is wandering.   A bill
for fifteen thousand francs."

"Embarrassing.   So you tried to sneak out and they
caught you?"

Old Nick raised his eyebrows.

"My dear boy, do you seriously suppose I could be as
crude as that?   No, I gave the situation a few moments of
intense thought, and then—the waiter had moved away—
I put a napkin on my arm and stepped across to a neigh-
bouring table where a fellow who looked like an Argentine
or a Greek or something of that sort was entertaining a lady
whom he was plainly trying to impress.   I presented plate

and bill to him. With a careless glance at the latter, he threw on the former a pile of notes. I thanked him, put notes, plate and bill on my table, and sauntered out. This morning the police were round here, making an absurd fuss. They gave me till tomorrow to find the money."

"Which by thrift and industry you have done."

"Precisely. It is as though a great weight had rolled off my mind. I feel gay, debonair, full of what your dear mother used to call the party spirit. Let us go out and revel. Or had you other plans?"

"I'm going to bed."

"To *bed*?"

"Have you ever travelled on a slow train across France on the hottest day of the summer?"

"Ah, I see. Yes, of course you must be worn out. You have taken a room in this pesthouse?"

"They call it a room."

"Probably worse than this one. The curse of poverty! Well, I won't keep you up. You are tired, and I must be off. You're sure you won't come along?"

"Quite sure. All I want is to lie down and forget."

"Then I will leave you. Pleasant dreams, my dear boy," said Old Nick, giving his tie a final adjustment in the mirror.

3

Terry, pushing her way through the crowds, had arrived at the Public Amusement Gardens. She found them much changed, so much changed, indeed, that their best friend would scarcely have known them. Normally, they are quiet and decorous, these Public Amusement Gardens, even to the point of dullness. Children walk in them with their nurses. Circumspect lovers whisper in them. Old gentlemen sit in them, reading the *Figaro* or *Le Petit St.*

Rocqueois. Their whole aspect lulls the observer to a stodgy calm: and, hearing their name, you cannot help feeling that St. Rocque must be easily amused.

Tonight, all was very different. Tables and waiters and bottles had broken out on every side like a rash. A band was playing with bulging eyes on the platform in the centre, and around this platform, in many cases far too closely linked, pirouetted the merrymaking citizenry, stepping high, wide and plentiful.

But the prediction of Armand the floor waiter that a hundred partners would leap into action the moment Terry presented herself in their midst was not fulfilled. The Public Amusement Gardens were congested with representatives of St. Rocque's *jeunesse dorée*, but they were all obviously involved with their own personal lady friends, and it was not long before Terry, wearying of the spectacle and finding that the din was making her head ache, decided that peace and quiet would be preferable. A stroll on the dunes, where there would be soothing darkness and a sea breeze to play on her face, suggested itself.

As she turned to go, something solid bumped into her. It was an elderly but well-preserved gentleman of aristocratic mien, who bared his head in courteous apology.

"*Mille pardons, mademoiselle.*"

"*Pas du tout, monsieur.*"

"Ah, you are American!" said the elderly gentleman, smiling a charming smile. "How your accent strikes a chord in my memory! My dear wife—my first wife—dead these many years, poor soul, was . . ."

He would no doubt have spoken further, for he was plainly in chatty mood, but at this moment Terry was swept away on a wave of revellers who with linked arms were surging to and fro to the considerable inconvenience of all. One of them was brandishing a pair of trousers. They passed on their way, and Terry, feeling like W. S.

Gilbert's Lord Lardy, 'How strange are the customs of France!' resumed her progress toward the dunes.

It was even darker on the dunes than she had expected. So dark was it that she could see nothing before her, and when a voice—almost, it seemed, at her elbow—spoke suddenly from the blackness, she leaped a liberal six inches and came to earth quivering. Until that moment nothing had given her to suppose that she was not alone in the silent night.

"Hoy!" said the voice.

Terry was a sweet-natured girl, but even sweet-natured girls can be ruffled. The shock had made her bite her tongue, and she spoke with a good deal of asperity.

"Who's that? You scared me stiff," she said, though fearing that the rebuke would be wasted on what was presumably an untutored Frenchman.

The voice uttered a whoop of joy.

"Gosh! For Pete's sake! Are you American?"

"I am."

"Thank God! I thought I should have to explain the situation in French, and I only know about two words of French."

"What situation would that be?"

"I'm in a spot. It's like this . . ." A sudden alarm seized the voice. "Hoy!" it said. It seemed to be its favourite word. "You aren't coming any closer, are you?"

"Not if you don't want me to."

"You see, I haven't any pants on."

"Any *what*?"

"Pants. Trousers."

Terry was conscious of a quick thrill. She was a girl who liked things to be interesting, and she found this human drama into which she had stumbled fraught with interest.

"Why not?" she asked.

The question, reasonable though it was, seemed to touch an exposed nerve in the voice. It barked in an over-wrought manner.

"I'll tell you why not. Because a bunch of drunks tore them off me. I was strolling along, minding my own business and not interfering with anyone, and they ganged up on me."

Terry remembered.

"Good heavens. I've met them. The trousers, I mean. In the Public Amusement Gardens. A man was dashing around waving them like the banner with the strange device Excelsior."

"I'd give him Excelsior, if I could catch him. I've been lurking on these damned dunes for hours, waiting for someone to come along."

"And here I am. What can I do for you?"

The voice seemed to reflect.

"It's difficult. I want to get back to my yacht."

"Oh, you have a yacht?"

"Lying in the harbour, and there are twenty-seven pairs of trousers of mine aboard her," said the voice in a tone of wild regret. "My name's Carpenter."

"Oh, yes. I've heard of you. You're a friend of Chester Todd."

"Do you know Chester?"

"By sight."

"Then everything's fine. He's sure to be around some-where. Would you mind hunting for him and telling him to get a boat and bring it here? Then he can row me to the yacht."

"Why, of course. I'll do it at once."

"I'm giving you a lot of trouble."

"Not a bit," said Terry. "Glad to help."

But when she had returned to the Public Amusement

Gardens, it became evident that the process of finding Chester Todd was likely to be a longer one than she had anticipated. He was no doubt, as Mr. Carpenter had suggested, around somewhere, but he was certainly not in the Public Amusement Gardens. Presumably he and Jo, shunning the vulgar mob, were dancing at one of St. Rocque's eleven hotels. Or at one of its fifteen restaurants. Or at one of its two Casinos. The prospect of having to visit all these places of entertainment, one after the other, chilled her.

It was as she stood wondering what to do for the best that she observed at a near-by table the distinguished-looking elderly gentleman with whom she had so recently passed the time of day and hurried toward him, feeling that this was where she did something constructive. He was not Chester Todd, but she saw him as one of those just-as-good substitutes.

"Excuse me," she said.

Old Nick was in a mood of quiet happiness. The lights, the music and the comfortable bulky feeling of the fifteen thousand francs in his hip pocket had combined to give him the illusion of being back in the days of his prosperity, when lights, music and money had played so large a part in his life. One thing only, he had just been thinking, was needed to complete his sense of *bien-être*, and that was the company of a charming member of the opposite sex. And now that essential ingredient had been added.

"I don't know if you remember me?" said Terry.

"Of course, of course. How could I forget you?" said Old Nick in a polished, paternal sort of way. "I have just ordered a bottle of champagne. Won't you sit down and join me?"

Terry shook her head.

"I'm sorry. I'm on an errand of mercy."

"I beg your pardon?"

"A human soul in distress. There's an unfortunate waif out on the dunes there who hasn't any trousers on."

Old Nick blinked. These were deep waters.

"Why not?" he said.

"Exactly what I asked him myself. It was the first question that shot into my mind. Apparently some revellers removed them from his person and went off with them. Don't ask me what the thought was behind it. I suppose it seemed a good idea at the time. So he's there waiting for someone to come along in a boat and rescue him, and I was wondering if you would help out. It would be a kindly act on your part."

A cold, non-co-operating look hardened Old Nick's handsome face, the look of a man who, no matter how eloquently Beauty may plead, is firm in his intention not to play ball. His attitude was understandable. This, unless you counted the deplorable Blamont-Chevry affair, was the first real night out he had had for months, and he did not propose to waste the golden hours rowing about in the darkness hunting for *sans-culottes* to whom he had never been introduced. And he was about to clothe this sentiment in words, when Terry went on.

"He wants to get back to his yacht. He has twenty-seven pairs of trousers there, which he seems to consider ample."

Old Nick started.

"His yacht? He has a yacht?"

"Big steam yacht. It's in the harbour."

The Public Amusement Gardens flickered before Old Nick's eyes. There was only one yacht in the harbour which could be so described, that of Frederick Carpenter, majority stockholder in the celebrated sparkling table-water, Fizzo, and the thought that he had been on the verge of refusing to succour and place under an obligation a young man worth—so he had read in his *Le Petit Rocqueois*

—a matter of twenty million dollars nearly gave him an attack of vertigo.

"Did he . . . did he tell you his name?" he said, when he was able to speak.

"His name's Carpenter. Not as of even date, of course, because at the moment it's mud. He's feeling pretty low, poor dear, and if you were to get a boat and row along the dunes shouting 'Mr. Carpenter! Mr. Carpenter! Come out of there, Mr. Carpenter, the United States Marines have arrived', I'm sure he would appreciate it."

"I will go without an instant's delay," said Old Nick, and was off like a jack rabbit, his heart singing within him. A grateful multimillionaire was what he had been scouring the country for for years.

4

It was in light-hearted mood that Terry made her way back to the Hotel Magnifique. She had hoped for an entertaining evening, and nobody could say that St. Rocque had not given her one. Only when she slipped silently in and found her sister Kate sitting here, bolt upright in a pink dressing-gown, did her exuberance diminish. She foresaw an unpleasant quarter of an hour, and was not astray in her prediction. It was precisely what she got.

Having accepted meekly a lecture which would have been considered on the severe side by a Hebrew prophet in the habit of rebuking the sins of the people, she ventured to inquire after Jo, and learned with surprise that the latter had returned an hour ago.

"It was that that woke me," said Kate. "She came in and knocked over a chair, and then she went to bed without a word."

"Without a word?"

"Well, she said she had a headache. I'm not surprised."

"But Jo never has headaches. I don't like this. Something must have gone wrong with her and Chester."

Kate uttered an elder-sisterly cry of concern. All these weeks she had been fearing the worst, and here it was.

"You think this man Todd insulted her?"

"Of course not."

"How do you know? We know nothing of him. He may have kissed her!"

"Well, what's wrong with kissing? The early Christians used to kiss everyone they met. Probably the trouble was that he didn't kiss her. I wonder if she's awake."

"She soon will be," said Kate, rising like a storm cloud. "Josephine!"

"Yes?" Jo's voice had a peevish intonation in it.

"Josephine, come here!"

"I'm asleep."

"Come here—immediately, Josephine," thundered Kate, and Jo came out, looking hostile.

Kate wasted no time in courteous preliminaries.

"What happened between you and Mr. Todd tonight?"

"Nothing happened. We had dinner and danced, and then I came home."

"Did he see you home?"

"Of course he did."

"In his car?"

"In a taxi."

Kate's worst suspicions were confirmed. She knew all about taxis.

"Did he kiss you?"

What sounded like the bursting of a paper bag competed with the din of the Festival. It was Jo laughing a hollow, mirthless laugh.

"He did not," she said. "How can you suggest that a respectable, upright married man would do such a thing?"

Terry squeaked in amazement.

"*Married?*"

"Been married for years. Jane Parker. Apparently she's a famous violinist and keeps her own name. He's a sort of Prince Consort. Mister Jane Parker. She plays the violin, and he plays second fiddle, ha, ha. So never mind about those two weeks, Terry, I shan't need them. . . . Well, good night, all," said Jo, speaking like a voice from the tomb. "If you are interested in my immediate plans, I'm taking the first plane home I can get, and I'm going to marry Henry."

She went back into her room, banging the door, and a silence followed her departure.

"Well," said Kate, breaking it, "I'm glad that one of you has some sense. Now we can all go home."

Terry shook her head.

"I'm not going home till I've seen Roville."

"What on earth do you want to see Roville for?"

"Nobody should miss it, so they tell me. The Jewel of Picardy, they call it, and the Mecca of the Fashionable World. And I've a feeling that something wonderful will happen to me there."

"Bah!"

"Just a hunch. I'm psychic."

"Pah!"

"You wait," said Terry.

5

Some two hours later, at the Pension Durand down by the harbour, Old Nick burst into his son's room and roused him from a deep sleep with an urgent hand on his shoulder.

"Jafe!"

Jeff sat up with a groan. The mists clearing from his

eyes, he was able to perceive that his parent was in a state of
extreme agitation and, like Kate, he feared the worst. He
blamed himself for having allowed this volatile man to run
around loose on such a night.

"Oh, heavens, Nick! What's happened now? What's
wrong?"

"Nothing is wrong. Everything is very much all right.
Do you know where I have been spending the last two hours,
Jafe? On a yacht. On a luxurious yacht lying in the
harbour, the property of Frederick Carpenter, the Fizzo
millionaire."

Jeff sighed.

"Nick, you've been drinking. Let me see you walk
across the room in a straight line."

"I refuse to walk across rooms in straight lines," said Old
Nick with a flash of the Maufringneuse pride. "Not that
I couldn't do it, and with the greatest of ease. You seem
sceptical, Jafe. Well, let me put a simple case to you.
You are a millionaire who has lost his trousers."

"I'm a *what*?"

"Good gracious, boy, can't you understand words of one
syllable? You are rich beyond the dreams of avarice, but
you have no trousers on."

"Why not?"

"Never mind why not. Suffice it that you have been de-
prived of your trousers and are lurking on the dunes,
earnestly hoping that somebody will arrive in a boat and
simplify the situation. I arrive in a boat. I announce my
presence by shouting. I row you to your yacht. In such
circumstances, would you not take me to your bosom,
would you not grapple me to your soul with hoops of steel?
Of course you would. And so did Frederick Carpenter—
or Butch, as he has asked me to call him."

"Why Butch?"

"A nickname bestowed on him at his university. He

was a great footballer, it seems. Yes, his gratitude was touching."

"And talking of touching——"

"Certainly not," said Old Nick, with hauteur. "I am not saying that a weaker man with his finances in the state in which mine are might not have tried to negotiate a small loan, but I kept my head. I introduced myself. I admired the yacht and deplored the whim that had led me to sell my own, for, as I told Butch, the salt of the sea was in my blood and there was nothing I enjoyed more than a yacht cruise. It was enough. A moment later he was inviting me to become his guest. We sail three days from now, which will give you ample time to return to Paris for your things and settle up your affairs."

"Me?"

"You are included in the invitation."

"But how about my work? I can't drop it to go gadding about on yachts."

Old Nick snorted impatiently.

"What nonsense! You will have plenty of leisure for your writing. Though why you want to write is more than I can understand. Writers are the most dreadful bounders. I've seen them in cafés in Paris, down-at-heels, inky fellows with scrubby beards. Still, if you must, you must, I suppose. No doubt it comes from having a mother who was an artist. Your mother was always messing about with those pictures of hers. I don't think I ever saw her when she was not covered with green paint. But you will be able to write as much as you please. You'll come?"

A vision of his hot, stuffy room in the Rue Jacob rose before Jeff's mental eye. It was followed by a vision of the sort of yacht that might be expected to house a sparkling table-water millionaire.

"Yes, I'll come."

"Good. Our destination is Roville, a delightful place as I remember it. We shall not live on the yacht. It will be there if we want it, but Butch is putting us all up at the Hotel Splendide. We shall be quite a small party, I understand. Just ourselves, a Mrs. Pegler, an American woman and her niece, a Miss Todd. Miss Todd's brother Chester and his wife were to have been with us, but they want to stay on a little longer in St. Rocque. And mark how all things work together for good . . ."

"Chester Todd?" said Jeff. "I know him. His wife is a violinist. I interviewed her once for the Paris *Herald-Tribune*, and he and I saw quite a lot of one another. He and his sister own some sort of table-water."

"Indeed? Like Butch. These table-water millionaires seem to stick together. But mark, I was saying, how all things work together for good. Where could I find anyone more suitable than a grateful Butch to supply the capital for my Umbrella Club? Naturally I did not mention the subject tonight—the time was not ripe—but an opportunity is sure to arise in the next few days. Well, I must not keep you up any longer. Good night, my dear Jafe. I will leave you to your slumbers."

6

On the yacht *Belinda*, Freddie Carpenter, smoking a last pipe before retiring for the night, was joined by his friend and guest, Chester Todd.

"Hi," said Chester.

"Hoy," said Freddie.

"Did you look in at the Festival?" asked Chester after a pause.

Freddie quivered.

"Did I look in at the Festival? You betcher I looked in

at the Festival, and do you know what happened?   The natives pinched my trousers."

"You don't say?"

"That's what they did.   Went off with them."

"Embarrassing.   What did you do?"

"I hid on the dunes.   I might have been there still, if a girl hadn't come along and fetched an old boy who fetched a boat and rowed me to the yacht.   A splendid old boy. We got along fine.   I've invited him to come to Roville with us."

Chester looked dubious.

"You're taking a chance, aren't you, inviting strangers on board?   He'll probably steal the spoons."

"Oh no, this guy's all right.   He's a Markee."

"French, you mean?"

"Yup."

"Then you watch those spoons closely, Butch.   I wouldn't trust a French Markee as far as I could throw an elephant."

"What do you know about French Markees?"

"I know them from soup to nuts.   My Aunt Hermione married one.   You should hear her on the subject.   Cancel the invitation, is my advice."

"I can't.   I wouldn't hurt Old Nick's feelings for the world."

Chester started.

"Old Nick?"

"He asked me to call him Nick."

Chester coughed.

"His name," he said, "isn't by any chance Nicolas Jules St. Xavier Auguste, Marquis de Maufringneuse et Valerie-Moberanne?"

"That's right.   He gave me his card.   Why, do you know him?   Who is he?"

"Only Aunt Hermione's former husband, whom she

cast into outer darkness where there is wailing and gnashing of teeth. She hates his insides. And you know Hermione Pegler. When she dislikes someone, she doesn't hide it in a gentlemanly way, she broadcasts it. You're going to have a very pleasant trip, my lad, with those two aboard. You'll feel like Noah trying to keep the tiger from chewing up the hippopotamus. Well, good night," said Chester, "I think I'll be turning in."

CHAPTER FIVE

ROVILLE-SUR-MER stands on the shore of the English Channel, and in Paris and other French centres you see a good many posters on the kiosks urging you to take your summer vacation there. They all speak very highly of the place.

Like so many of the popular seashore resorts of France, Roville started out in life as a modest fishing village, inhabited by sons of the sea in blue jerseys who, when not fishing, played interminable games of boule on the waterfront. Then progress hit it. The boule arena is now the mile-long Promenade des Anglais, there are two Casinos, and large white hotels stand gleaming wherever you look—notably the Carlton, the Prince de Galles, the Bristol, the Miramar and—most luxurious of all—the Splendide. Roville points with pride at the Hotel Splendide, and with reason. It has all the latest improvements, including an American bar presided over by Philippe, formerly of Chez Jimmy, Paris, a first-class orchestra and cuisine, a garden for the convenience of guests wishing to commit suicide after visiting one or other of the Casinos, and ruinously expensive suites, mostly on the first floor, with balconies looking over the water.

Terry was on the balcony of her first-floor suite this morning, standing at the rail and looking down at the beach. The golden sands dotted with striped umbrellas—you get a suggestion of them on the posters—made an attractive picture, but it was with a discontented frown that she eyed the scene, and the frown was still on her face as she turned and went back into the suite to talk to Kate.

"Kate," she said, "I'm bored."

"Who wouldn't be?" said Kate.

"I suppose you aren't enjoying this any more than you did St. Rocque."

"I'm hating every minute of it."

"So am I," said Terry. She paced the room restlessly. "It's this thing of not being able to get to know anybody that's breaking me down. I always thought you were all one great happy family at these places, but we've been here nearly a week, and we haven't met a soul. Apparently when it goes to Mecca, the fashionable world keeps itself to itself. If you want to be one of the gang, you have to have letters of introduction. I feel like someone in an old English novel, who is being cut by the County. I wonder Dale Carnegie doesn't write one of those How To books of his about this beastly place. How To Come To Roville And Not Feel Like A Leper. How To Lure The Best People Into Occasionally Throwing You A Kind Word. How To Obtain An Introduction To A Dark Young Gentleman With Brown Eyes And A Scar On His Cheek Who Looks Like Gregory Peck."

"*What!*"

Kate sat upright and rigid. She was fearing the worst again.

"Who is this man?"

"Which man?"

"The man with the scar on his cheek."

"Oh, just someone I've seen around the hotel. I thought he looked interesting."

"Has he spoken to you?"

"Don't be silly, woman. This is Roville. You don't speak to anybody here unless they're endorsed by a couple

of Bishops and a Dame of the British Empire. Oh, gosh,"
said Terry. "How I miss Jo!"

"If you had any sense, you would do as she has done and
go home."

"I hate to be beaten."

"Tchah!"

"Still, there's a lot in what you say.   Shall we go home?"

"You know how I feel about it."

"All right, then, that's settled. We go home."

"When?"

"As soon as you like. And meanwhile I'll be taking a
refreshing swim.   It will help to pass the time."

2

On the terrace of the Splendide, a vision in gleaming
white with a panama hat on his shapely head, Old Nick
was in conversation with his son Jefferson. He was making
his first public appearance, for a chill, caught on the voyage,
had kept him confined to his bed for the last few days.
Old Nick always took his minor ailments seriously.

"Most extraordinary coincidence," he was saying, returning to a subject which had engaged his interest many
times since the yacht *Belinda* (F. Carpenter, owner), had
left St. Rocque. "It makes one uneasy. It gives one that
uncomfortable feeling that you can never know, as you go
through life, what is going to jump out at you next. When
you met her, could she have knocked you down with a
feather?"

Jeff admitted that he had been somewhat taken aback.

"I, too," said Old Nick. "For a moment my aplomb
left me entirely. It was the complete absence of any kind
of warning that unmanned me. 'A Mrs. Pegler,' Butch
said. I was aware, of course, that after we parted your

stepmother became Mrs. L. J. Quackenbush, but how was I to know that she had divorced Quackenbush and married this Pegler, whoever he is? Though I suppose I ought to have realized that she was a woman who would seldom let a day pass without divorcing someone. Shortly before our marriage she had severed relations with a man named Vokes, and I am not sure if even he was the first on the long list."

Jeff hazarded the theory that getting divorced was habit-forming, like opium or cocaine.

"You think one more divorce won't hurt you and after that, you say to yourself, you'll quit. But the craving still grips you. You have to have another and another and another. You become an addict. Very sad."

"I see what you mean. You feel she is more to be pitied than censured?"

"If you take the broadminded view."

"One should always do that, of course. Still, I don't like it. When a woman who ought to be Mrs. L. J. Quackenbush suddenly appears calling herself Mrs. Winthrop Pegler, it seems somehow furtive and under-handed, as if she were going about under an alias. However, nothing to be done, I suppose, except to try to bear her society with fortitude. Not that that's easy. You always found her unsympathetic and hard, did you not?"

"Hard as nails. I remember reading somewhere of a woman of whom you felt that her skin was stretched on brass. I thought the writer must have met your late Marquise. It can't have been very pleasant, being married to her."

"Not very," Old Nick agreed. "Still, worse of course if one had been a spider."

"I'm not quite sure I follow you there."

"Spiders have the most trying married lives. Old Soupe at the bureau collects them and studies their habits.

The moment the honeymoon is over, he says, the female spider eats the male spider."

"She does?"

"So Soupe tells me."

"Oh, well, if there's nothing else in the house . . ."

"I admit Hermione stopped short of actually eating me—one must give her credit for that—but, as I was saying, I found the years of our union not easy ones to live through."

"I've often wondered——"

"Yes?"

"Oh, nothing.   I forget what I was going to say."

Old Nick sat up alertly, like an actor who has received a cue.

"You were going to say you have often wondered why I married her. I will tell you. I did it for your sake, my boy, so that you should have every advantage in life," he said nobly. "I married in order to be able to support you in luxury. And what happened? The minute I'd done it, you ran away from home. You rendered my efforts null and void by suddenly disappearing one day without a word and going off to America."

"It seemed the best thing to do. She made it pretty clear that I wasn't needed. So that was why you married her, was it? You grudged me nothing, no matter what the cost to yourself?"

"Exactly. And now it is your turn."

"Oh, Nick!"

"It's no use saying 'Oh, Nick!'"

"If you're trying to hound me on to woo Mavis Todd——"

"Did I mention Mavis Todd?"

"No, but there was a gleam in your eye when you introduced us."

"The gleam has faded. Nothing doing in that quarter, I fear. She's going to marry Butch."

"Are they engaged?"

"Not yet, but one can see that Hermione is straining every nerve to bring it about. Of course, if you were to make a special effort——"

"No, thank you."

"Perhaps you're right. No good expending nervous force and energy on a hopeless project. She's an odd girl. I wish she would sometimes say something except 'Yes, Auntie'."

"I've heard her say 'No, Auntie'."

"Indeed? Still, you would not call her a sparkling conversationalist."

"Butch isn't, either. I'd say she was just right for Butch."

"Soulmates?"

"That's the word."

"I am inclined to agree with you. A curious fellow, Butch," said Old Nick, pursuing a train of thought. "He has a strange kink which I have noticed in several of his wealthy countrymen. In many ways lavishness itself—I have certainly no complaint to make of the hospitality we are enjoying at his expense in this hotel—he has a parsimonious streak in him. He came to see me the other night as I lay on my bed of pain, and I felt the moment had arrived to broach the subject of my Umbrella Club. He agreed to finance it without a murmur. Whatever capital I might require, he said, I could have. He was like a mediæval monarch distributing largesse. Yet next day he was in the depths of gloom. On leaving me he had gone to the Casino and lost some quite trivial sum at the roulette table. You would have thought from his demeanour that he was one of those fellows who lose their all and reach for their revolvers and . . ." He paused. He saw that he was not holding his audience. Jeff was gazing into the middle distance, a rapt expression on his face.

"You aren't listening," he said testily. "What's the matter?"

Jeff started.

"I'm sorry. I just happened to see that girl go by. Off to take a swim. Extraordinary," said Jeff, "how attractive she looks in a wrapper."

"What girl is this?"

"Her name's Trent, they told me at the desk—she's American."

Old Nick quivered at the magic word. Americans were always rich. God bless America, he had often felt, unconsciously plagiarizing the poet Berlin.

"She has a suite on the first floor."

Old Nick quivered again. He knew what those suites on the first floor of the Hotel Splendide cost.

"Looks a nice girl," said Jeff carelessly. "I've seen her about the place. I've wished occasionally that there was some way of getting to know her."

"Some way?" Old Nick's voice trembled. "There are a hundred ways of getting to know girls at a seashore resort."

"Such as——?"

"Save her from drowning."

"She'd be much more likely to save me. She's a wonderful swimmer. I've—er—happened to see her once or twice. But she goes out too far, much too far," said Jeff earnestly. "It's dangerous. Suppose she got cramp? It makes me anxious. Any other suggestions as to what I could save her from? Fire? Runaway horse? Assassins?"

"Don't treat this thing with levity," said Old Nick severely. He was still thinking of that suite on the first floor. "I don't like to feel that a son of mine is lacking in enterprise. Get into conversation with her—casually, as it were."

"She's not the sort of girl one gets into conversation with casually, as it were."

"Then you had better leave it all to me."

"What can you do?"

"A thousand things."

"Name three."

"One will be sufficient. You say she is on her way to swim. I will take a boat and follow her."

"Mixed bathing?"

"Nothing of the kind. I shall row up and warn her that there is a storm coming on. She will climb gratefully into my boat, and—*voilà tout!* By the time we get ashore, we will be like ham and eggs, as your mother used to say."

Jeff regarded him with an admiration which he did not always feel when he contemplated this good old man.

"You have a great brain, Nick."

"So people have told me."

"I believe it would work."

"It always used to."

"She wouldn't snub a man of your age."

"What do you mean, a man of my age? A man is as old as he feels, and I feel about twenty. But how do I recognize her?"

"It won't be difficult. She has a face like a Botticelli angel, a scarlet bathing cap with wisps of fair hair peeping out from under it like little rays of sunshine, blue eyes with the sort of warm glow in them that you see in a summer sky, teeth like pearls, a lovely mouth, beautiful arms, a perfect figure and a nose that turns up slightly at the tip with two small freckles at the end of it," said Jeff simply. "You can't miss her!"

3

It was some three-quarters of an hour later that Mrs. Wintrop Pegler came on to the terrace of the Hotel Splendide, accompanied by Frederick Carpenter and her niece,

Mavis Todd. She was a handsome, severe woman with elaborately waved hair and plucked iron-grey eyebrows, who looked like an elderly Gibson girl with something on her mind. And there was a good deal on her mind. She was brooding on her former husband, the Marquis de Maufringneuse, and his son Jefferson.

The emotions of Mrs. Pegler on being introduced to Old Nick aboard the yacht *Belinda* had been even more poignant than his when introduced to her. He had been merely startled. She had experienced the sharp horror which she would have felt if, when walking through some sunlit meadow, she had found a serpent in her path. For his presence—in white duck trousers, a blue coat with gold buttons and a yachting cap—had told her that there was a plot afoot, a sinister plot designed to undo all the patient spadework with regard to Freddie Carpenter and her niece Mavis which she had been putting in since shortly after Christmas.

Through one or other of her discarded husbands . . . possibly Vokes, possibly Quackenbush . . . Hermione Pegler had acquired substantial holdings in both Fizzo, the sparkling table-water controlled by Freddie Carpenter, and Clear Spring, the sparkling table-water controlled by her niece Mavis Todd and Mavis's brother Chester. She was naturally anxious to see these holdings increase in value, and as nothing so spruces up the value of sparkling table-water shares as a merger between the two leading rival concerns, she was resolved to promote this merger. And obviously the marriage of Mavis and Freddie would be an ideal first step to such an end.

And everything had looked extremely promising until on their arrival at St. Rocque Old Nick had suddenly popped up from nowhere, full of subtle schemes and patently planning to weave them.

She knew Old Nick. None better. She knew him as a

man who, learning by who could say what dubious means
that there was a girl with a vast fortune aboard a yacht in
the harbour, would lose no time in insinuating himself into
the good graces of the owner of that yacht, in wheedling
out of him an invitation to join the party and then sending
for that son of his. Hoping, of course, that the latter,
exercising his spells, would carry on from there.

And he had every ground for such a hope. She disliked
Jeff extremely, but she did not blind herself to the fact that
he was a singularly attractive young man, just the sort of
young man—with his dark good looks and that romantic
scar on his cheek—in whose hands Mavis, who was virtually
an imbecile, would be as wax. Thank heaven, she felt,
grateful for small mercies, that the child had been seasick
all the way from St. Rocque, so that nothing had happened
during the danger period of the voyage.

Musing thus, she crossed the terrace and at a table in the
corner perceived Old Nick, in close conversation with a
fair-haired girl in a Dior summer dress. They seemed to be
getting along splendidly.

Old Nick's recognition of Terry and Terry's recognition
of him, when he rowed up in his boat with the courtly
'Pardon, mademoiselle' which had always gone so well at
seashore resorts in his bachelor days, had been mutual and
instantaneous. Neither, once seen, was easily forgotten.

"You!" said Old Nick. "Well!"

"Well, well!" said Terry.

"Well, well, well!" said Old Nick.

She had climbed into his boat, though scoffing at the
suggestion that there was a storm coming up, and they had
returned to shore, prattling gaily. Back on dry land,
Terry had gone to dress, and they were now enjoying a
drink and talking about Old Nick's son Jefferson.

"You may have seen him about the place," said Old
Nick. "He has a scar on his cheek."

"What!"

"An honourable scar, a scar any father might be proud of. He got it in the Maquis."

"Where's that?"

"The Maquis. The French Resistance. He shed his blood for France, shed it profusely. And he is as gifted as he is brave," said Old Nick, forgetting his scorn of authorship in the effort to give his offspring the build-up which is always so essential on these occasions. "He writes novels and things. His mother was an artist. Painted pictures and things. I suppose that's where he gets it from. Certainly not from my side of the family."

It was at this moment, as Terry sat with her heart racing and her eyes shining, so it seemed to Old Nick, like twin stars, that Mrs. Pegler, Freddie and Mavis came up.

"Oh, here you are," said Mrs. Pegler without pleasure, addressing her former consort.

Terry was still in a dream as Old Nick, leaping up lissomely, did the honours.

"Miss Trent, Mrs. Pegler. Her niece, Miss Todd. Mr. Carpenter, our host. Miss Trent and I met at St. Rocque the night of the Festival. And this will interest you, Butch. She was your angel of mercy."

"Eh?"

"It was she who informed me of your predicament that night. I was sitting in the Public Amusement Gardens, thinking of this and that, when she came up and told me of the bereavement you had suffered."

"Gosh!"

"Upon which, of course, I immediately hurried off and sped to the rescue."

Mrs. Pegler spoke. For some moments she had been drinking Terry in with a glacial eye, a dark suspicion burgeoning in her bosom.

"That was your first meeting with Miss Trent?"

"We bumped into one another a few moments earlier in the crowd."

"I see. Just a casual acquaintance."

There was nothing glacial in the eye with which Freddie was drinking in Terry. He gazed at her enraptured. He was a large young man with bright red hair and a freckled face.

"So you were that girl? I don't know how to thank you, Miss Trent. Trent?" said Freddie, knitting his brow. "Yes, I remember now. I met a Miss Trent at dinner one night in St. Rocque. Any relation?"

Terry could feel her toes curling and she was conscious of the breathlessness which had attacked her that night at Bensonburg when she had stood in the garden looking at the new moon, but she replied composedly.

"I have no relations in St. Rocque. In fact, I don't think I have any relations in the world except my cousin, who is here with me, and a sister in America," she said, and for the first time was thankful that Jo had left her. If Freddie had encountered in Roville as Fellowes the maid a girl whom he had encounted in St. Rocque as Miss Trent, an embarrassing situation would unquestionably have arisen. "Did you find your twenty-seven pairs of trousers when you got back to the yacht, Mr. Carpenter?" she asked, changing the subject.

"Eh? Oh, yes. Yes, they were all there all right. And talking of the yacht, would you care to see it?"

"I should love to."

"Let's go," said Freddie.

A silence followed their departure. It was broken by Mrs. Pegler, who was looking grim.

"Mavis!"

"Yes, Auntie?"

"Go and look at the shops."

"Yes, Auntie."

"I want to have a word in private with the Marquis."

"Yes, Auntie."

"Just a brief word, Nicolas," said Mrs. Pegler, as her niece drifted off. "I wonder . . . is it possible," she said, eyeing him fixedly, "that you think I don't see what you are up to?"

Old Nick was all courteous interest.

"Up to, my dear?"

"That was what I said."

"I'm afraid I don't understand, my dear."

"Let me enlighten you," said Mrs. Pegler in a metallic voice. "I should hate to think that you think I think——"

"Start again."

"I should hate to think that you are under the impression that you are pulling the wool over my eyes. There is something almost laughably transparent about you, Nicolas."

"Not about you, my dear. You speak in riddles."

"I will make myself plainer. You're going to try to marry that son of yours to Mavis."

"Ridiculous!"

"And in order to divert Frederick and take his mind off Mavis you have produced this girl who calls herself Miss Trent——"

"It's her name."

"It may be her name. That has nothing to do with it. It's entirely obvious what sort of a girl she is . . . running around St. Rocque unescorted, letting you pick her up. . . ."

Old Nick swelled portentously.

"Are you impugning Miss Trent's honour and respectability?"

"Yes."

"Well, you shouldn't," said Old Nick, who could be very severe on occasion.

"I could see at a glance that the girl is an adventuress."

"My dear!"

"And don't keep calling me my dear. My name is Mrs. Pegler."

"A sad come-down from Marquise de Maufringneuse et Valerie-Moberanne."

"On the contrary, a distinct step up. But that is immaterial. What I want to say to you is this. I intend that Frederick shall marry Mavis, and unless you give up this plot of yours——"

"Plot? What plot?"

"Nicolas, please. Do you think I don't know you? My good man, we're not strangers. I lived with you for years. How I did it, I can't imagine, but we need not go into that. The point is that if you don't call off that precious son of yours and get rid of this girl, I shall expose you to Frederick. I shall tell him you're just a seedy old deadbeat and fortune hunter without a red cent to your name except what you can cadge from people dumb enough to be taken in by that title of yours, as I was," said Mrs. Pegler, descending to the personal. There are moments when only the most nervous prose will serve.

"Think it over, Nicolas," she said.

Old Nick laughed a jolly laugh.

"But, my dear, I mean my dear Mrs. Pegler, you don't suppose that Butch does not know all about my circumstances? Immediately after meeting you on board the yacht it occurred to me that it would never do to accept his hospitality under false pretences, so I was quite frank with him, making no secret of the fact that the exchequer was low. The revelation left him quite indifferent. He had a moment of uneasiness when he wondered if I was really a Marquis, but when I assured him that I was, and offered the Almanac de Gotha in proof, everything was hotsy-totsy, as my first wife used to say. So don't go to all the bother of exposing me. Just a waste of time."

It was some moments after Mrs. Pegler had left him,

giving him a long, lingering look of the if-looks-could-kill type as she did so, that Old Nick became aware of a small boy at his elbow, a boy in the uniform of the Hotel Splendide, which is a little like that of a Field-Marshal in the Ruritanian army. In his hand was a salver, on the salver a telegram.

Old Nick opened it, and frowned.

WHERE IN THE NAME OF TEN THOUSAND DEVILS IS THE DOSSIER QUIBOLLE?—DE LA HOURMERIE

He crumpled it up and threw it petulantly under the table, annoyed at this intrusion of sordid office matters into his carefree holiday. What a pest this man De La Hourmerie was, to be sure, with his eternal dossiers Quibolle. Fussing, fussing, fussing, always fussing . . .

Then, as he thought of his recent triumph over the forces of darkness, his equanimity returned. The cloud cleared from his face and he was his radiant self again.

He beckoned the waiter and ordered another visky-soda.

4

Having inspected Freddie Carpenter's yacht and returned to the hotel, Terry paused for a moment on the front steps to look at the view.

The spectacle before her eyes . . . yellow sands, sapphire water and out on the horizon mysterious islands wrapped in a pearly mist . . . was one which she had always appreciated, but this morning it had a new magic. The sands were more golden, the water bluer, the islands more than ever like something out of a fairy story. For Terry was in love, and love sharpens the vision.

Only twenty minutes ago . . .

A young man in the dining-saloon hammering away at a typewriter. Freddie apologetic.

"Oh, hello, Jeff. Afraid we're interrupting you."

"Quite all right."

"I'm showing Miss Trent the yacht. Miss Trent, the Comte d'Escrignon."

And that was how it had all begun.

Terry went up to the suite. Kate was there, reading the Paris *New York Herald-Tribune*. It reached Roville at about noon, and was balm to her homesick heart.

"Did you have a good swim?" asked Kate.

"Splendid," said Terry. "And I've met the young man who looks like Gregory Peck. He's a Count."

"He would be!"

"Well, he has to be, because his father's a Marquis."

Kate sniffed. She had her own opinion of French Marquises.

"He seems quite nice," said Terry, and went into her room to get ready for lunch, conscious of having abbreviated her story a little. She had not, for instance, mentioned what had occurred when Freddie, called away for a moment on one of those mysterious yacht-owners' errands, had left her alone with Jeff and she had seen that look in his eyes, had seen him coming slowly toward her, had found herself in his arms, kissing Jeff, being kissed by Jeff, a Jeff who had become very French and was murmuring things like 'Je t'aime' and 'Je t'adore' . . .

One didn't tell Kate everything.

Still, there was something one had to tell her.

"Oh, Kate," she said, opening the door, "I'm not going home."

"What!"

"No, I've changed my mind. I misjudged Roville. Roville," said Terry, "is all right."

CHAPTER SIX

PIERRE ALEXANDRE BOISSONADE, Commissaire of Police, sat in his office in the Rue Mostelle, a great bull of a man with a red, accordion-pleated neck and beetling eyebrows. He was interviewing a caller who had called to request official permission to carry firearms.

With regard to this commissaire there were two schools of opinion in Roville. One—of which he was the sole representative—thought him a good fellow, a *bon enfant*, and in his dealings with the general public courteous and obliging almost to a fault. The other—more numerous—credited him with the disposition of a snapping turtle and manners which would have been considered brusque by Simon Legree or Captain Bligh of the *Bounty*. After five minutes of his society the caller, who was a meek little individual of the name of Floche, had joined the second group. The Commissaire had just observed that he had no time to waste listening to him, M. Floche, and that if he, M. Floche, would be good enough to turn his head, he would see the door behind him.

"But I desire a permit to carry a pistol. You can give it to me, can you not?"

"No."

"Why not?"

"Because I don't want to," said Pierre Alexandre Boissonade with the air of a man on a quiz programme who has answered an easy one.

M. Floche became plaintive.

"But I live in a dangerous part of the town."

"Move elsewhere."

"It is not safe there after dark, and my profession makes it necessary for me to be out late at night. I play the clarinet in a hotel orchestra."

"Stop playing the clarinet. Adopt another profession."

"Find me one."

"This is not an employment agency."

"And if some apache attacks me?"

"I shall then authorize you to carry a pistol."

"After I have been massacred by the apache?"

"Precisely."

"I never heard anything so silly in my life," said M. Floche.

The Commissaire gave him a look.

"That is enough," he said sternly. "Under the orders of the government which I have the honour to serve, I am here to carry out the laws, and not, as you appear to imagine, to discuss their wisdom. If you don't like the laws, change them."

"I wish I could! I spit myself of these crazy laws."

"What? What? One word more, my fine fellow, and I arrest you. Coming spreading revolutionary sentiments in the very office of the Commissaire! Was there ever such effrontery? Out of here! Out of here, Anarchist, before I . . . Monsieur Punez!"

"Sir?"

"Remove this person."

The unhappy Floche, not waiting to be removed, melted away, thinking dark thoughts, and the Commissaire turned menacingly on his subordinate, a man in the fifties who looked, as subordinates of commissaires like Pierre Alexandre Boissonade are apt to look, older than his years.

"Monsieur Punez, a word with you. I have the honour to inform you, Monsieur Punez, that you are a fool and an

imbecile, and that, if you continue to perform your duties as
you have been doing, I shall ask the Prefect to request your
resignation.   How often, Monsieur Punez, have I told you
to attend to these trivial matters yourself?   Pistol permits!
What idiocy!   Am I to occupy myself with pistol permits?
And now I suppose you have come to tell me that somebody
else has called to waste my time?   Well, who is it?   Someone who has been insulted by a taxi-driver?   A cook
claiming a week's back wages?   The bereaved owner of a
lost dog?   Don't stand there twiddling your fingers,
Monsieur Punez.   Speak, idiot!"

"There is a lady, sir.   A Madame Pay-glare."

"What does she want?"

"She did not say, sir."

"Well, don't let her in."

"What do you mean, don't let me in?" said Mrs. Pegler,
entering like a galleon under full sail.   "That's a nice way
to run an office.   You're the Commissaire, aren't you?"

"I am, madame."

"Well, then I want to see you," said Mrs. Pegler, taking
a seat with the brisk firmness of one who has come to stay.

M. Boissonade threw his arms out in a despairing
gesture and raised his eyes toward the ceiling, as if asking
Heaven why it allowed a good man and a *bon enfant* to be
persecuted like this.   His voice quivered.

"You want to see me!   Ha!   About your husband, of
course?   You have come to lodge a complaint against your
husband, *hein*?   Why is it that all women have this rooted
idea that the Commissaire is a mender of broken homes?
Let me inform you, madame, that domestic disturbances
do not fall within the province of a commissaire of police.
Except in cases of flagrant infidelity, when a husband has
introduced a concubine into the conjugal circle, the Commissaire has no power to intervene.   Has your husband
introduced a concubine into the conjugal circle?"

"Ay-coot-ay, moose-yer——"

"Please! No useless words. Yes or no? If yes, complain to the Parquet, and I shall receive my instructions. If no, kindly withdraw."

"Moose-yer . . ."

"Enough. I see it now. You are about to say that your husband beats you. Very good. In that case, have the offence testified to by witnesses, produce the evidence in the divorce court, and the judge will see to it that your pleas receive a hearing. But don't come bothering *me*. The obsession you women have that the Commissaire can handle these affairs! *Sacrébleu!*" said M. Boissonade, still addressing the ceiling. "It is insupportable. If I were to intervene, olive branch in hand, in all the homes where there is domestic trouble, I would need months of sixty days and days of forty-eight hours. You exasperate me, madame. I am *bon enfant*, but when women come wasting my time——"

"Oh, shut up!" said Mrs. Pegler.

Actually, for she was speaking the painstaking French which she had learned at her finishing school, she said 'Tay sayvoo', which is not quite so abrupt as 'Shut up'. But it was abrupt enough to stir M. Boissonade to his depths. Removing his gaze from the general direction of Heaven, he fixed on Mrs. Pegler the same awful stare with which he had quelled M. Floche.

"Madame!"

"It's got nothing to do with my husband. My husband is in America. If you'll kindly stop talking for a moment, if you know how, I will tell you what I've come for."

The flame in M. Boissonade's eye died to a mere flicker. He relaxed. He did not like Mrs. Pegler's manner—very few people did—but what she had said had soothed him. 'America' was the operative word. He held the simple creed of the French official, that all Americans are made of money and that some of it generally sticks to the fingers of the man who does them a service. It was impossible for him to look kindly and benevolent, especially in the morning before he had had his lunch, but he looked as kindly and benevolent as he could manage.

"Pray, proceed, madame," he said, cooing not exactly like a dove in springtime, but with a certain resemblance to such a bird.

Mrs. Pegler hesitated.

"This is confidential."

"Perfectly, madame."

"It won't go any further?"

"I assure you, madame."

"Well, then, this is how things stand. You've probably heard of Mr. Frederick Carpenter. He owns that big yacht that's in the harbour."

"Ah, yes. The rich American."

"That's right. Well, I want him to marry my niece."

"Indeed, madame?"

"I've gone to a lot of trouble to bring them together, and I was hoping pretty soon to get results. But now——"

"There has been a quarrel? A misunderstanding?"

"Of course not. Mavis hasn't brains enough to quarrel with anybody. No, what has happened is that a girl has appeared on the scene and is doing her utmost to alienate Mr. Carpenter's affections."

"Zut!" said M. Boissonade, all sympathy and concern. His look seemed to suggest that it was a revelation to him that human nature could sink so low. "Who is this woman?"

"She calls herself Trent, and she's got a suite at the Splendide."

"Ah!"

M. Boissonade had a solid respect for persons rich enough to occupy suites at the Splendide.

"Naturally she has to put up a front," said Mrs. Pegler correctly interpreting his emotion, "but anyone can see she's an adventuress. I knew the moment I saw her there was something fishy about her, and I want you to find out what it is. It may be bad enough so that you'll be able to run her out of town. That suite of hers is probably full of faked passports and things. Go take a look. Get the goods on her."

M. Boissonade started. This was big stuff.

"You suggest that I send one of my men to search this woman's suite?"

"No, I don't. I suggest that you do it yourself. I don't want the whole of the Roville police force in on this."

A flush darkened M. Boissonade's face. He had a keen sense of the dignity of his position. And he was about to correct Mrs. Pegler's apparent idea that commissaires of police were private eyes, when she went on.

"I'll give you five hundred dollars."

M. Boissonade gulped. His eyes rolled, and the ends of his moustache jerked. He was aware that he was being insulted, but his attitude toward insults was much the same as that of Pooh-Bah in *The Mikado*. He sat silent for a moment, working it out in francs.

"Well?"

M. Boissonade came out of his reverie. He had done his sum, and he liked the look of it.

"I shall be very happy to oblige Madame," he said simply, and Mrs. Pegler said that was all right, then, and what was the procedure?

"Do you have to have a search warrant?"

"No, madame."

"But you can't just walk in and start hunting around."

M. Boissonade smiled faintly.

"Naturally one will use finesse. One will wait until the suite is empty, a simple matter to arrange."

"It doesn't sound simple to me."

M. Boissonade permitted himself another smile.

"Madame is forgetting that this woman who calls herself Tur-rente is unaware that she is under suspicion. She is confident, at her ease. She little knows . . ." He paused. He had been about to say, 'She little knows that Commissaire Boissonade is on her trail,' but felt it was perhaps too florid. "That the police are interested," he substituted. "Are you on cordial terms with this woman?"

"No."

"But sufficiently friendly for you to be able to invite her to dinner?"

"Oh, I see what you mean." Mrs. Pegler's face cleared. "I ask her to dinner, and while she's out, you slip in?"

"Precisely. Does she live alone?"

"There's someone with her she calls Kate. Another obvious adventuress."

"Invite them both, and select a restaurant at some distance from the town, so that there will be no danger of their premature return. I would suggest the Grenouillière at Aumale. It is fashionable, and it is a drive of thirty kilometres."

"Now you're talking," said Mrs. Pegler. "Now you've said something."

She looked at him with admiration. At the outset of their interview she had had this commissaire docketed as a stuffed shirt and a broken reed, but she saw him now as a man of infinite sagacity and resource, in whose hands she could place her affairs with every confidence.

She rose and made for the door, and the Messrs. Floche and Punez, who for the last ten minutes had been resting their ears against the keyhole, sprang nimbly back and went their respective ways, M. Punez to his desk, M. Floche to the sunshine of the street outside.

2

Well, really, Old Nick was saying to himself as he trotted along to his son Jefferson's room that afternoon, in even the most hard-boiled specimens one often finds a surprising amount of hidden and unsuspected good. The conversation he had just had with the former Marquise de Maufringneuse had restored his faith in human nature. It had also startled him considerably. If anyone had told him five minutes before that he was about to receive an invitation to dinner at an expensive restaurant from a woman from whom the best he would have expected would have been the offer of a dose of weed-killer, he would have scoffed at the idea. But the miracle had happened, and he hastened to Jeff's room to tell him about it.

The sound of a typewriter coming through the door as he approached it made him purse his lips, and it was with a disapproving frown on his face that he entered.

"Do I interrupt you, Jafe?" he asked with a touch of coldness.

"You do," said Jafe cordially. "What's on your mind?"

"A rather extraordinary thing has happened. Your stepmother has invited you and me and Miss Trent and that cousin of hers to dine tonight at the Grenouillière at Aumale. Amazing, is it not? I think she must have had some kind of a change of heart. Something has softened her."

"Heard an organ playing one of the songs she loved as a child, do you think?"

"Very possibly. She was positively amiable. Said there was nobody who could order a dinner like me and would I attend to all the arrangements. It's the first civil word she has spoken to me since our honeymoon. I was astounded."

"I don't wonder."

"I propose to let myself go regardless of expense, as she will be paying the bill. Caviar, I think, followed by Bisque d'Écrevisses, Truite à l'Archduc, Perdreau Perigourdin, Asperges and . . . well, and so on. Naturally I have not thought the whole thing out yet, but I can assure you that it will be a feast for the gods. You'll come, of course?"

"I'm sorry. I can't. I'm dining with a man."

"Put him off."

"I haven't the heart. He was so pathetically anxious for my society. He arrived this morning from St. Rocque. Chester Todd. Mrs. Pegler's nephew, if you remember."

"Of course, yes. The brother of that extraordinary silent child with the large eyes. But surely he will be at the dinner?"

"No. His aunt doesn't know he's here. He begged me to keep his presence dark for the moment. I gather that he feels he needs a cheerful night out before he starts fraternizing with her."

"I don't blame him. Well, that's too bad. Still, there it is."

"There it is, Nick. And now will you kindly vanish. I've work to do."

"Work? Work? All this talk of work!" said Old Nick, who looked on work as a form of nervousness. "It's ridiculous that you should be sitting in here scribbling on a lovely afternoon like this. You ought to be out in the sunshine with Miss Trent."

"Yes."

"Playing tennis with Miss Trent."

"Yes."

"Swimming with Miss Trent. Boating with Miss Trent."

"Yes."

"Well, why aren't you?" said Old Nick, with the air of a counsel for the prosecution cornering a shifty witness.

Jeff sighed.

"I wonder if Erle Stanley Gardner has to go through this sort of thing when at his desk," he mused. "No, probably not. He couldn't turn out sixteen books a year if he did. What's the use of talking about playing tennis with Miss Trent, and swimming with Miss Trent and being out in the sunshine with Miss Trent, Nick? You're only encouraging patricide, which, let me tell you, is a very bad thing and frowned on by the Law. I am dodging Miss Trent, Nick, avoiding Miss Trent, using every effort not to be left alone with Miss Trent—whether in or out of the sunshine."

Old Nick gaped.

"But I understood you to say that she attracted you."

"The word is inadequate."

"She does attract you?"

"She does, Nick."

"Then I fail to understand your attitude."

Jeff sighed again.

"It's quite simple. Why waste my time and hers? What have I to offer her?"

"The name of a Maufringneuse."

"And the income of a Maufringneuse."

"You must not think so much of money, my boy."

"I'm sorry. It's a family failing, I suppose. But the fact remains. She's rich, and I'm a hard-up hack, so the whole thing's impossible."

"But, Jafe——"

"It's no good talking, Nick. When it comes to marriage, I'm pure Potter. I'm not going to beg any girl to support me. I'm conscientious."

Old Nick winced. He knew, of course, that conscientious men existed, but it was not nice to have to hear about them.

"You have disappointed me, Jafe," he said, with a dignity that became him well.

"I'm sorry. Well, see you later, Nick, drop in any time you're passing," said Jeff, and resumed his hammering of the typewriter.

It was a saddened and depressed Old Nick who wandered out on to the terrace and took a seat under one of the striped umbrellas. His was the old, old tragedy of the father who cannot understand his son.

He found Jeff's attitude incomprehensible.

It was not as though the boy were in the position of having to nerve himself to a distasteful task, as had happened to some of his ancestors. Several Maufringneuses in the past had had a thorny path to tread where their matrimonial ventures were concerned. There were in the family portrait gallery—or had been till they were sold—pictorial representations of earlier Maufringneuse brides with faces well calculated to stop any clock, for it is seldom in an imperfect world that wealth and feminine allure go together. Yes, those ancestors of his, quite a number of them, had come up the hard way. They were Maufringneuses and had thought of the girl's money and set their teeth and done the big, brave thing, but it could not have been at all pleasant for them.

But Jeff had no such obstacle to surmount. His rich young woman was a beautiful and charming rich young woman, and on his own confession he was deeply enamoured of her. And yet from some ridiculous Potter scruple he hung back. One can hardly wonder that Old Nick, having summoned a waiter, ordered in place of his customary visky-soda a half-bottle of champagne. When the heart is really bowed down with weight of woe, only

Mumm, Bollinger and the Messrs. Perrier and Jouet can pick it up again.

He had drained his glass and refilled it and was sitting dreamily watching the beaded bubbles winking at the brim and beginning to feel a little better, when abruptly all the good the excellent wine was doing him was undone by what sounded like the explosion of an ammunition dump in his immediate rear.

"WHERE," inquired M. de La Hourmerie, for it was he, "is the dossier Quibolle? WHERE is the DOSSIER QUIBOLLE?"

It was at this moment that Kate came on to the terrace. The afternoon was warm, and she thought she would like a lemonade, or, as they called it in this deplorable country, a citronade. The first thing that met her eyes after she had taken a seat under one of the striped umbrellas was Old Nick, a few tables away, in an animated conversation with a small, stout man of pug-dog appearance whose head was swathed in bandages.

3

Ever since her talk with Terry on the day when the Marquis de Maufringneuse and his son, the Comte d'Escrignon, had come into their lives, Kate had been a prey to uneasiness, apprehension and concern. An adept at reading between lines and smelling rats, she had found her suspicions awakened by Terry's change of mind in the matter of shaking the sand of Roville off their shoes and going home. It was a change of mind that had given her furiously to think.

For if, she reasoned, a girl says she wants to go home and then, immediately after meeting a young man with dark eyes who looks like Gregory Peck, says she would prefer not to, it means something. And it was an elder sister's duty, she considered, to inquire into the financial status of this Peck-like young man.

She very much doubted if it would bear inspection. If she had read one magazine story where the foreign aristocrat turns out to be a penniless impostor, she had read a hundred. Her feelings with regard to Old Nick and his son were, in a word, precisely those of Mrs. Pegler with regard to herself and Terry. Mrs. Pegler, pouring her troubles into the sympathetic ear of Commissaire Boissonade, had spoken of adventuresses. Kate was thinking in terms of adventurers.

The only trouble about inquiring into the financial status of adventurers is that it is so difficult to find a reliable source of information. Ask the adventurers themselves how they are fixed for money, and they freeze you with a stare. Ask their friends, and the friends probably know nothing more than they have been told by the adventurers. It was this problem, amounting to an impasse, that was harassing Kate as she sat sipping her citronade, and it was as she wrestled with it, seeking for a solution, that she observed Old Nick and the man with the bandaged head.

She watched them with a growing feeling that here perhaps was the source of information of which she was so sorely in need. It was plain to an observant eye that the man with the bandages knew Old Nick well, but his whole bearing and deportment made it clear that he did not look on him as a friend. One had only to see the way he shook his fists and danced rudimentary dance steps to know that whoever at some future date he might nurse in his bosom, it would not be the Marquis de Maufringneuse et Valerie-Moberanne. They were too far off for their conversation to be audible, but anyone with Kate's ability to read the language of gesture could have no doubt that the Marquis de Maufringneuse et Valerie-Moberanne was being called some extremely offensive names and told precisely where he got off.

For a time the scene, as these scenes so often do, appeared likely to last for ever; but suddenly Old Nick, who had been listening with the courteous attention of a polite man hearing a dull story which he has heard many times before, gave his companion what looked like an encouraging pat on the shoulder and went off into the hotel. What had happened was that, taking advantage of a momentary shortness of breath on M. de La Hourmerie's part, he had said that he had an idea that the dossier Quibolle might be among his effects in his room and that he would pop upstairs and have a look for it. He disappeared, and M. de La Hourmerie, puffing slightly after his exertions, slumped into the vacated chair and reached out for the glass of champagne on the table. Dorothy Dix or any good authority on etiquette would have told him, of course, that considering the names he had just been calling Old Nick, it was scarcely the done thing to help himself to the latter's wine, but M. de La Hourmerie was beyond the reach of authorities on etiquette. And the golden nectar had just begun to trickle down his throat, when he was aware of Kate standing at his side.

"Oh, you poor man," said Kate.

Womanly sympathy, she felt, was the right opening gambit. You can't beat womanly sympathy.

M. de La Hourmerie's initial impulse, for though his thoughts were unpleasant, he wished to be alone with them, was to hurl the glass at this intrusive female, but it still had some champagne in it and the prudent man does not waste a drop. He contented himself with glaring like a short-tempered basilisk.

"Did you have a motor accident?" said Kate.

The desire to confide overcame M. de La Hourmerie's exasperation. He had in no way modified his view that what Kate needed was to be skinned with a blunt knife, and subsequently dipped in boiling oil, but it is an exceptionally determined man who, when his head is in a cocoon of bandages, can resist the urge to blazon forth to the world the events leading up to these bandages.

"I did not," he said curtly; "I was hit on the head with a hatchet."

"What!"

M. de La Hourmerie gave her a nasty look. 'You heard,' he seemed to say.

"You don't mean it!" said Kate, clucking like a hen.

"Then perhaps you will inform me," said M. de La Hourmerie, always a handy fellow with the swift retort, "what I do mean. I repeat my statement. Somebody hit me on the head with a hatchet."

"Gracious!"

"A glancing blow, because the fool let the weapon slip in his hand. You would think that if you were going to murder someone with a hatchet, it would be perfectly simple to make a good job of it, but no. Sloppiness! Inefficiency! The curse of the Civil Service," said M. de La Hourmerie broodingly.

Kate continued to cluck.

"Who was this man?"

"One of my clerks. Fellow named Letondu."

"But why did he do such a thing?"

"Because he's a raving lunatic. Some nonsense about a shining figure appearing to him and telling him to start wiping out the heads of the various departments, beginning with me. The whole thing's absurd. I don't suppose a shining figure ever so much as said a word to him."

"No wonder you're upset."

"Upset?" The inadequacy of the word caused M. de La Hourmerie to explode, as if he had been stuffed with

trinitrotoluol and some hidden hand had touched it off.
"I'm a persecuted man. First that pig of a Marquis——"

Kate welcomed the introduction of Old Nick into the
conversation. She had been wondering how best to lead
up to him.

"I saw you talking to the Marquis," she said.

"*I* talked to him," said M. de La Hourmerie with gloomy
satisfaction. "Oh, yes, I talked to him. Going off with
the dossier Quibolle in his pocket. . . ."

"I beg your pardon?"

"The dossier Quibolle," said M. de La Hourmerie,
raising his voice. "He took it away with him that day at
the bureau when I sacked him."

"But I don't understand. Was the Marquis in your
employment?"

"For years he was. At least it seemed like years. One
of my clerks, and the worst I ever had."

"One of your clerks? Then he isn't rich?"

"Idle, inefficient, never at the office, and when he was
at the office, going about with that sickening smile on his
face . . . Rich? No, of course he isn't."

"But his château in the Ardennes?"

"Sold years ago. Everybody knows about the Marquis
de Maufringneuse. Married an American millionairess,
and she divorced him. He hasn't a penny."

"Well!" said Kate, filled with the stern joy of the
woman who is in a position to say 'I told you so', and at
this moment Old Nick returned, full of courageous apology.

"My dear fellow," said Old Nick, "what must you
think of me?"

M. de La Hourmerie in a brief passage reminded him
that he had already mentioned what he thought of
him.

"I've just remembered that I left the dossier Quibolle
at my rooms in Paris. You'll find it in the top left drawer

of the chest of drawers, under my handkerchiefs. The concierge will let you in. Mention my name, and say I sent you. It might be as well to slip the fellow a few francs."

M. de La Hourmerie stood for a moment gazing fixedly at Old Nick, then, as if feeling that no words at his command could do justice to the situation, turned and moved away. And Old Nick was about to sit down and resume his communion with the champagne, when a cold female voice said "I should like to speak to you, Marquis", and he found Kate confronting him.

Kate's lips were drawn in a thin, tight line, and there was a steady glitter in her eye. She reminded Old Nick of one of the eighteenth-century Marquises de Maufringneuse, the third on the left as you entered the family portrait gallery, whose menacing glare had haunted him since boyhood.

4

Jeff had struck a difficult patch in his novel, and the thought crossed his mind, when Old Nick came bursting in as he sat wrestling with it, that there was a good deal to be said for the life of the orphan. With no fathers constantly darting in on them like rabbits, orphans can manage to get some work done. However, he was a dutiful son and concealed his annoyance as he turned to greet the intruder.

"Hello, Nick," he said. "Back again? You do keep popping up, don't you?"

It was only then that he observed that his parent's normally unruffled features were drawn and twisted and and that he was breathing heavily like a man whom some sling or arrow of outrageous fortune has struck on a tender spot.

"What on earth's the matter?" he asked, concerned. "Have you met one of your creditors?"

Old Nick puffed like a grampus.

"Jafe, an appalling thing has happened. Miss Trent. It's terrible. I'm shaking in every limb."

Jeff's face whitened.

"Is she hurt?"

Old Nick seemed puzzled.

"Hurt? Of course not. Who would hurt her?"

"She hasn't had an accident?"

"Not to my knowledge. In the pink of condition, as far as I know."

"Then what do you mean," demanded Jeff wrathfully, "by scaring the life out of me like this? I thought you were going to tell me she had been run over by a truck or something."

"There are worse things than being run over by trucks, my boy," said Old Nick gravely. He paused, uncertain whether to break it gently or not, and came to the conclusion that this was no time to beat about bushes and break things gently. "I've just been talking to that cousin of hers," he said. "She's found out about our financial position. She knows exactly how we stand—that I am penniless and you also. And prepare yourself for another shock, my boy. Miss Trent is penniless, too."

"What!"

"Penniless!" repeated Old Nick, sepulchrally. "She owns a third share in a chicken farm over in America, and that is all. Not a very big chicken farm either, I gathered."

"But what's she doing in a suite at the Hotel Splendide?"

"Apparently she recently became possessed of a small sum of money—a legacy, presumably—and decided to spend it on a jaunt to Roville. One sees what was in her mind, of course," said Old Nick, who would have done just the same thing if he had been a girl. "She hoped to catch a rich husband. What a merciful dispensation of Providence it was that enabled me to discover this before you had definitely committed yourself! I am not a religious man, but really there are times when one cannot help having the feeling that one is . . . how shall I put it? . . . *protected*."

He broke off, startled by the cry that burst from his child's lips. A Soul's Awakening look had come into Jeff's face. If Old Nick had been Clutterbuck telling him that after talking it over with his partner Winch he had decided to add his novel to their autumn list, he could not have betrayed a greater ecstasy.

"But this is wonderful! This is splendid. This makes everything all right. Now we can get somewhere. If she's as broke as I am——"

Old Nick shook from stem to stern.

"You aren't proposing after this to ask her to marry you?"

"What else do you think I'm proposing to do? I'm going to write her a note asking her to come and have dinner somewhere tomorrow, and the moment the coffee has been served and there isn't a waiter hanging around with flapping ears listening to everything we say, I shall . . . well, I shall know what to do about it."

"My boy, I entreat you!"

Jeff looked at him, surprised.

"Don't you like the idea?"

"I think it's terrible. You can't marry a pauper."

"Of course I can. Watch me. Brush up your dance steps, Nick, because you'll soon be dancing at the wedding. I can't imagine what you're making all this fuss about," said Jeff, the Potter strain in him definitely uppermost. "You say she's got no money. All right. What of it? And I've got no money either. Well, what of that? What's wrong with being hard up if you love each other? It's fun. Everything becomes an adventure. A new hat for her is an achievement. The dreams, the plans, the obstacles that must be surmounted—the rich don't have any of that."

"No," said Old Nick with spirit, "and they don't have to pig it in an attic up six flights of stairs."

Jeff did not allow this thought to discourage him.

"I want an attic up six flights of stairs. With a candle by the bed. When you blow out the candle, you make believe you're in a room at Versailles with silk hangings and cupids dancing on the ceiling. That's life, Nick, that's living."

Old Nick was staring at him, aghast.

"Good God!" he gasped. "You're a blasted poet!"

At any other time Jeff would have denied the charge hotly, but he was too busy now pacing the floor and snapping his fingers.

"You've probably noticed how her nose turns up at the tip?" he proceeded, deeply moved. "And those two little freckles on it. Have you considered what it will be like having those permanently about the home?"

"And have you considered," said Old Nick, rallying, "that now she knows you are a poor man, she won't look at you?"

"She'll look at me."

"I consider it most unlikely. If I were in her position, I would erase you from my thoughts and marry someone with millions, like Butch."

"But then you're an old devil, Nick, without any of the finer feelings. Butch, forsooth! Terry wouldn't marry Butch for his money. She's pure gold. If she let me down, I'd turn my face to the wall and give up the struggle."

"But, Jafe——"

"Leave me, Nick," said Jeff. "I would be alone. I have to concentrate on that note. It wants wording just right."

Old Nick, who, following the advice he had once given

M. de La Hourmerie, normally walked with a springy step,
was shuffling—even tottering—as he made his way down to
the hotel lobby.   Jeff's lyrical outburst had shocked him to
the depths of his Maufringneuse soul.   No man who be-
lieves that marriage should be a sound commercial trans-
action devoid of all sickly sentiment likes to feel that he is
the father of a son who appears to be the Last of the
Romantics.   Slowly he walked down the stairs and slowly
crossed the lobby to the American bar of which the Hotel
Splendide was so proud.

There, placing a shapely foot on the brass rail, he
requested Philippe, formerly of Chez Jimmy, Paris, to start
mixing him one of his justly celebrated Specials.

5

It was about a quarter of an hour later that Old Nick,
feeling somewhat refreshed, though still weak at the knees,
came out of the American bar and, crossing the lobby,
encountered Terry, who had been swimming.

He found himself eyeing her askance.   Fond though
he was of her, and he could recall few girls to whom he had
taken a more immediate liking, it was impossible for him to
feel that if you examined the matter squarely and without
bias, she had betrayed a good man's trust.   Nobody who
looked as rich as she did and occupied suites at expensive
hotels had, in his opinion, a right to turn out to be the one-
third owner of a small chicken farm on Long Island.   Sly,
he considered it, and deceitful.

However, there was nothing in his manner to indicate
how deeply his feelings had been wounded and how sadly
his faith in American womanhood shaken.   He kissed her
hand with his customary courtliness and said how delighted
he was to think that they would be meeting that night.

"Mrs. Pegler tells me you have accepted her invitation to dinner."

"Yes," said Terry. "I'm looking forward to it. It will be fun dining out in the country. This Grenouillière place is quite a place, isn't it?"

"It has a great reputation."

"Who will be there?"

"One or two acquaintances of Mrs. Pegler's, I understand."

"Your son?"

"No. Jafe is dining with a friend."

"Oh?" said Terry, and tried to keep flatness out of her voice. "Freddie Carpenter, I suppose?"

"No, he is dining here with Miss Todd. They are going to a concert."

"Still, you will be there."

"Yes, I shall be there."

"Well, that's all a party needs to make it a success, isn't it?" said Terry, and with a bright smile continued on her way upstairs.

Kate was still out when she reached the suite, and she was glad not to find her there. She wanted to be alone, to give an uninterrupted mind to a problem which had been tormenting her since that day on the yacht, the problem of Jeff and why he was acting in such a peculiar way.

His attitude bewildered her. On the rare occasions when they found themselves alone together, he had been extremely polite, meticulously courteous, but always with a reserve that amounted to aloofness. Never a suggestion on his part that anything beyond the small change of conversation had passed between them. It was as though what had been to her the supreme moment of her life had been to him just a casual episode, meaning nothing.

And probably, she felt bitterly, that was exactly how he regarded it. She had been naïve enough to attach importance to those kisses, those broken trembling words, not realizing, poor idiot, that he probably kissed every girl he met who was not a positive gargoyle and threw in broken, trembling words for good measure. Frenchmen were like that, butterflies flitting from flower to flower. Probably he had forgotten the whole thing ten minutes later. Probably he had platoons of mistresses all over the place. Probably this 'friend'—ha!—he was dining with tonight was one of them, some horrible little *cocotte* called Fifi or Mimi or some such repulsive name, with high heels and lots of ribbons and lace who would address him as 'Chéri'.

She was just thinking hard thoughts of this impossible creature and harder ones of Jeff, when his note was brought to her by the same juvenile Ruritanian Field-Marshal who had brought M. de La Hourmerie's telegram to Old Nick. She opened it, and instantaneously the whole aspect of what had been a pretty inferior sort of world changed in a flash. The sun shone out. An unseen orchestra started to play soft music. Roses and violets came popping up through the carpet. And Jeff, who a moment before had been an unpleasant blend of wolf and worm, sprouted wings and a halo.

She read the letter three times. It was short and in tone quite restrained, but it seemed to her a beautiful letter. She read it again and it seemed more beautiful than ever. She was reading it for the fifth time, memorizing every golden word, when the telephone rang.

The clerk at the desk informed her that two gentlemen had called and would be grateful if they could see her for a moment on a matter of importance.

6

The two gentlemen, presenting themselves some minutes later, were not very imposing gentlemen. One was a melancholy little individual with a spade-shaped beard, who looked as if he might be a clarinet player in a hotel orchestra, the other, who also gave the impression of having seen a good deal of trouble, stood perhaps six feet in his stout boots and had a drooping moustache. It was he who attended to the introductions.

"My name is Punez, mademoiselle."

"How do you do?"

"My brother-in-law, M. Floche."

"Good afternoon, M. Floche. Is there something I can do for you?" said Terry, with some difficulty restraining herself, for she was in expansive mood, from telling them she was going to have dinner tomorrow with the only man anyone could possibly want to have dinner with. At the same time she suddenly realized why it was that the appearance of her visitors seemed so familiar. Allowing for the beard and the moustache, they were exactly like Mutt and Jeff. Not her Jeff, the other one. Mutt continued to do the talking; Jeff seemed to be one of the silent sort.

"I am attached to the Roville police force, mademoiselle."

"Oh, yes?"

"I assist M. Boissonade, the Commissaire."

"Oh, yes?"

"Who is a pig and a bounder and a tyrant," said M. Punez with heat. "He is a *rogommier*," he added, an epithet new to Terry but one which she instinctively divined was not intended to be complimentary. She stored it up for future use. It would be a good thing to call Mr. Clutterbuck next time he started throwing his weight about with reference to the price of honey.

"He is plotting against your welfare, mademoiselle. We heard him, I and my brother-in-law, M. Floche. We were listening at the door throughout. Is it not so,

Hyacinthe?" said M. Punez, and M. Floche, who appeared to answer to that remarkable name, wagged his beard briefly, as much as to say You betcher (*tu parles bien*) it was so.

Terry was mystified. If she had been an international spy, with one eye always out for the police force of any country in which she happened to be, she would no doubt have taken this piece of information with a careless 'Oo là là' and a wave of a jewelled hand, but she was not an international spy.

"How do you mean, plotting against my welfare?" she asked, surprised that a commissaire of police of whom she had never heard should know she had a welfare, let alone plot against it.

"He is coming tonight to search your suite on behalf of a Madame Pay-glare."

Terry started. This began to make sense.

"You had better tell me all about it," she said.

M. Punez told her all about it. When he had finished, Terry was experiencing the emotions of some wayfarer in a thunderstorm on a dark night, to whom a sudden flash of lightning reveals that he is standing on the brink of a precipice. She bit a thoughtful lip, and her feelings toward Mrs. Pegler, never affectionate, hit a new low. It wounds a sensitive girl to learn that she has been asked to dinner solely with a view to getting her out of the way while the police go through her belongings.

"What do you think I ought to do?"

M. Punez had a ready answer. There was a vengeful gleam in his eye as he gave it. He had suffered much at the hands of Pierre Alexandre Boissonade.

"If I were Mademoiselle, I would ensure that some muscular male friend was present in readiness to receive the pig when he makes his entry. Springing upon him in the darkness, he would——"

"Give him a *marron*," said M. Floche, speaking for the first time.

"A *marron*?"

With a gesture M. Punez indicated that what his brother-in-law was advocating was that Mademoiselle's muscular male friend should bestow on the intruder a mouse, a shiner, a black eye, and Terry cordially agreed that this would be admirable in every way. It saddened her to think that Jeff, who would thoroughly have enjoyed this whiff of the old Maquis days, was not available to attend to the matter. But there was always Freddie Carpenter. She knew little of the ways of commissaires when searching suites, but she presumed that M. Boissonade's visit would take place at some fairly late hour, when Freddie would have returned from his concert. Yes, Freddie was the people's choice.

She beamed on M. Punez.

"I don't know how to thank you," she said.

M. Punez intimated modestly that he had only done what any man would have done—any man, he seemed to imply, who for years had been crushed beneath the iron heel of Pierre Alexandre and now saw a chance of getting a bit of his own back. His bearing had become quite sunny, and even M. Floche—what you could see of him behind the beard—looked considerably brighter. It was with something of the jauntiness of a couple of old-style vaudeville song-and-dance men doing a Shuffle Off to Buffalo to the O.P. exit, that a few moments later they took their departure, leaving Terry to muse alone on this surprising crisis in her affairs.

A vision of Freddie rose before her eyes, and she found it comforting. It was never long in his acquaintanceship with anyone before Freddie touched on the old college football days, and she had been fully apprised of how he had earned the sobriquet of Butch. It seemed to her that a former Princeton tackle was just what was required to instil into

Pierre Alexandre Boissonade the realization of how wrong it is to sneak into girls' suites at night and search them. Encountering fourteen stone of Frederick Carpenter in the dark would, she felt, prove a turning point in the life of Pierre Alexandre Boissonade, doing him all the good in the world. He would come out of the experience a graver, deeper commissaire. And she was just regretting that Mrs. Pegler would not be with him to get her share of the impending doom, when Kate came in.

Kate was looking triumphant, and no unprejudiced critic would have denied her right to do so.

"Well," she began, feeling far too stimulated to lead by easy stages into the big item on the agenda paper, "I've found out all about this precious Marquis and that son of his. As I suspected from the first, they're frauds. They haven't a penny to bless themselves with."

It would be idle to deny that Terry was startled. Her eyes widened.

"What!"

"I've been talking to the man who was the Marquis's boss in some Ministry or other. The Marquis was just one of his clerks, and he's not even a clerk now. He was fired."

"You mean he is not a Marquis?"

"Oh, I suppose he's that all right," said Kate, "but who isn't, in France? The point is, he's just another of these decayed aristocrats who haunt places like this, living on their wits. He hasn't any money at all."

Terry found herself recovering. Money? What did money matter? What did anything matter except that she was dining with Jeff tomorrow?

"And what is more," said Kate, "I told him exactly what your position is."

"You didn't!"

"I certainly did. I told the old man you hadn't a cent except what you could make out of selling eggs and honey.

I left him hurrying off like the White Rabbit in *Alice In Wonderland*, presumably to tell his son. You won't see much more of *that* young man, I fancy."

"I'm dining with him tomorrow night."

"You think you are. When did he ask you?"

"I had a note from him just now."

"Written, I'll bet, before he heard the bad news. You'll get another tomorrow, saying he's terribly sorry but something very important has come up and he's afraid he must cancel the date."

"I won't!"

"He's probably writing it now," said Kate, and went into her room to take her hat off.

For a long minute after she had gone Terry sat staring with eyes that saw nothing at one of the pictures on the wall, for in the first-floor suites of the Hotel Splendide there were pictures and everything, no expense spared. She was feeling rather as Pierre Alexandre Boissonade was going to feel when he met Freddie Carpenter tonight. Then suddenly the cloud lifted. The numbed sensation left her, and she was herself again. The absurdity of the idea that Jeff was the sort of man Kate had suggested made her laugh.

She was still laughing when she went into Kate's room.

"Oh, Kate," she said, "that dinner tonight. I'm not going."

Kate stared.

"Not going? What do you mean?"

"I won't be among those present."

"But you've accepted."

"I don't care."

"I can't go without you."

"Of course you can. Tell the Pegler woman I've a headache."

"She'll come inquiring."

"She won't. She'll get the dreadful news when she's thirty kilometres out in the country, where we're all going to meet.   Some English friend of hers is taking us in his car, as hers will be full.   He won't do any inquiring."

Kate sniffed.

"Well, I simply cannot understand you. It was only the other day that you were complaining of not knowing anybody."

"I'm like that.   Temperamental."

"What will Mrs. Pegler think?"

"What does it matter what she thinks? Give her a *marron*."

"A *what*?"

"And tell her it's from me," said Terry.

CHAPTER SEVEN

IT was late that night when Jeff got back to his hotel after his dinner with Chester Todd, as it usually was when those who dined with Chester Todd got back to their hotels. Chester was an amiable young man who, when his wife was not at his side to check his self-expression with a gentle hand, liked to throw himself whole-heartedly into the evening's pleasure. Tonight she was in Paris, for on the morrow she was giving a violin recital before a distinguished audience, and in her absence he had yielded unrestrainedly to the promptings of his generous nature. At about eleven-thirty, Jeff, having put him to bed, went to his room to take a shower. It was not until he had left the bathroom, feeling greatly restored, that he noticed that there was a letter lying on the table.

Inspection revealed that it had been forwarded from his Rue Jacob address, and the envelope suggested that whoever had written it was staying at the Ritz. Mystified, for he could think of no one in his circle of acquaintance opulent enough to patronize that hotel de luxe, he opened it, and his heart, as he saw the signature, leaped like a rocketing pheasant. He had not been so deeply and immediately stirred since the morning in his Maquis days when, calling at a farm in the hope of getting eggs for himself and friends, he had found the kitchen full of German soldiers with rifles on their laps.

He blinked. But when he opened his eyes, the signature was still there:

J. RUSSELL CLUTTERBUCK

He stood staring at it. Then it occurred to him to read the letter.

It was brief and business-like, the letter of a man to whom time is money. J. Russell Clutterbuck, it appeared, was in Paris for a few days and would like to have a talk with him. Would it be possible, J. Russell Clutterbuck wondered, for Jeff to join him at lunch at one o'clock on Wednesday. Wednesday, Jeff realized, as far as his dazed mind was able to realize anything, was tomorrow.

He collapsed into a chair and sat there, still dazed but capable now of reasonably coherent thought. And, brief though it was, Russell Clutterbuck's communication provided abundant food for thought, not so much in its actual contents as in what was between the lines.

Russell Clutterbuck would like to have a talk with him. Hold firmly to that thought, for that was where the interlinear material began. When busy publishers take the time to talk to young authors who have sent them their novels, they do not talk about the weather or the political situation. They talk about the novel and the profundity of their emotion when, on starting to read it, they were suddenly struck all of a heap and felt like some watcher of the skies when a new planet swims into his ken. It was absurd to suppose that Russell Clutterbuck wanted him, Jeff, to break bread with him, Clutterbuck, merely because he, Clutterbuck, was curious to see how he, Jeff, broke it. Obviously what he, Clutterbuck, had in mind was not a social get-together, but a business conference.

He was just thrilling at this thought, when he suddenly remembered that tomorrow was the day he was dining with Terry.

A good seventy per cent of his elation left him. But he had no alternative, he felt, but to cancel the engagement. He knew nothing of Russell Clutterbuck, except that he wrote wonderfully stimulating letters, but he presumed him to be a man with a sense of his own importance—a man, in fine, who might quite naturally take offence if a young author whom he was entertaining to lunch interrupted him in the middle of a sentence to say that he was sorry but he must be going now, as he had an appointment elsewhere. There was nothing to be done but write Terry a note.

What to say in the note was a difficulty. His impulse was to tell her all, to pour out to her all his hopes and dreams, but he was strong and resisted this temptation. Though not a particularly superstitious man, he felt that no good ever comes of taking things for granted and starting cheering before the battle is won. As Henry Weems would have put it, one must not count one's chickens before they are hatched.

The letter which he finally managed to assemble, always bearing this danger in mind, merely stated that he had been unexpectedly called to Paris and . . . for one never knew whether a beautiful friendship might not spring up between Russell Clutterbuck and himself, causing the former to keep him at his side for days . . . was unable to say when he would be returning.

He took it downstairs and left it at the desk. Then he rang up Freddie Carpenter and asked him if he might borrow his car tomorrow. In his uplifted frame of mind he found the thought of trains revolting. He wanted the old gipsy feeling of bowling along the high road at a high rate of speed, thinking long, dreamy thoughts of the girl he loved—and, of course, of Russell Clutterbuck.

2

At the moment when Jeff telephoned, Freddie Carpenter had been sitting on the balcony outside his suite, which, like Terry's, was on the Hotel Splendide's fashionable first

floor, looking at the moonlight on the water.   As soon as he
had hung up, he returned there and resumed his inspection.

His mood was lushly sentimental. How beautiful is
night, no mist obscures nor cloud nor speck nor stain breaks
the serene of heaven, he was saying to himself (or words to
that effect), and was conscious of strange emotions stirring
within his forty-four-inch bosom. He was thinking of
Mavis Todd.

Until an hour or so ago Freddie's feelings toward Mavis
Todd could best have been termed tepid. Asked to
describe her, he would have said that she was a nice little
thing, fairly pretty in her way but in no sense a knock-out,
one of those girls, in short, whom you can take or leave
alone—her most endearing quality the fact that, being
quiet and mouselike, she was an agreeable contrast to the
varnished-haired, wisecracking young women who had
paralysed him at so many a cocktail-party. For there was
nothing of the dashing playboy about Freddie Carpenter.
He was a shy young man and liked girls to be quiet, though
goodness knew that it was only once in a blue moon nowa-
days that you found one who was. Yes, Mavis had always
seemed to him quite tolerable—what dramatic critics call
adequate—but nothing more. She had never spoken to
the deeps in him.

Tonight everything was changed. The scales had fallen
from his eyes and he was seeing her as one equipped with all
the earmarks of a soulmate. He felt like some Californian
householder who, digging idly in his back garden, finds
with surprise that his spade has struck an oil gusher. It
was as though his guardian angel had tapped him on the
shoulder and whispered, 'Butch, you poor pinhead, are you
blind? Cannot you see that this is what you have been
looking for all your life?'

Right at the start she had made an excellent impression
on him by her ready acceptance of his suggestion that they

should duck out of that concert and go to the pictures.
Highbrow music, he said, gave him a pain in the gizzard,
and when Mavis revealed that that was precisely where it
gave her, too, a pain and that she had contemplated
attending the concert simply because Auntie had told her
to, Auntie holding the view that concerts have an educa-
tional value, he had felt for the first time that here was a girl
with something on the ball, a girl who would bear watching.

At dinner the discovery of a mutual dislike for shrimps
and a mutual admiration for the art of Agatha Christie
had helped things along quite nicely, but it was only when
she revealed that the Uncle George of whom she had spoken
once or twice in the course of conversation was none other
than the great Snake Todd that Freddie's mind had turned
definitely in the direction of matrimony.

Snake Todd was one of the fixed stars in the firmament of
football, a man whose name even after two decades had
passed was still breathed with all the awe it had evoked in
the thirties, and the thought that, if he played his cards
right, he too might one day be in a position to call this god-
like man Uncle George, so electrified Freddie that he
choked on his roast veal and had to have his back slapped
by a waiter. When his eyes had ceased to water, he turned
them on Mavis with such a wealth of passion that she in her
turn swallowed a mouthful the wrong way. The whole
thing would have reminded a Shakespearian scholar of the
first meeting between Romeo and Juliet.

It seemed to Freddie that if he had interpreted right that
swallowing-a-mouthful-the-wrong-way sequence and her
subsequent acquiescence when he had held her hand at the
pictures, the thing was in the bag. And what was so wonderful about it, he thought as he watched the moon in full-
orbed glory rolling through the dark blue depths, was that
she was as rich as he was, if not richer, so that if he succeeded in winning her, it would not be that blasted money

of his that had done all the heavy work. That was what made his eyes misty as he gazed at the silver ripples on the water, the thought that he was loved—if he was loved, and he was prepared to bet on it—for himself alone.

It was a totally new experience for him. Quite a number of girls in the last year or so had shown an up-and-coming cordiality in his presence, but always he had had the depressing feeling that it was not his personality that appealed to them so much as the fact that, owing to the public's generous support of Fizzo, he had more millions salted away than you could shake a stick at. Only now had there swum into his ken a member of the opposite sex who had not one bright eye fixed on his bank account.

Musing thus, he was roused from his reverie by the tinkling of the telephone in the room behind him, and for a moment was in two minds about answering it. It was probably, he thought, Jeff again, and fond though he was of him, he had no wish to talk to Jeff. He wanted to be alone with his dreams and visions. However, it being practically impossible to ignore a ringing telephone, he went to the instrument and barked into it an annoyed "Hello".

A soft voice came over the wire.

"Butch."

It was not Jeff. The voice was female.

"Mavis?" he murmured tenderly. "Is that Mavis?"

"No, it's me. Terry Trent."

"Oh, Terry? You're back, then?"

"Back where?"

"Back here. From the Peglers' dinner."

"I didn't go to the dinner. Listen, Butch."

"Yes?"

"I'm scared. I believe there's a burglar sneaking around."

"A what?"

"Burglar."

"Oh, burglar? Surely not? What makes you think that?"

"Just now the handle of the door turned slowly and mysteriously, as if someone were trying it."

And not a bad line to take, thought Terry. It had occurred to her that if she were to tell Freddie that she was expecting a midnight marauder to put in an appearance shortly, it would be difficult to make the thing sound plausible. Freddie was not the most astute of men, but even he might wonder how she came to be clairvoyante. A mysterious hand, slowly turning door handles, was better in every way.

"You see, I'm supposed to be out at Aumale, dining with Mrs. Pegler, so whoever it is thinks the suite's empty. I wish you would come over, Butch."

"Of course I will. Shall I dress? Eh? What did you say?"

Terry had not spoken. She had giggled. Feeling as she did in the highest spirits, she had only just stopped herself from assuring him that there was no need to dress, as the affair would be quite informal.

"Just come as you are."

"I'm in pyjamas."

"Well, stay in pyjamas," said Terry. "But come. Walk along the balcony. The window's open."

3

It was some minutes later that a cautious knock sounded on the door of her bedroom, and Freddie's voice spoke.

"Hoy."

"Yes?"

"Here I am."

"Good."

"But you must have been dreaming. There's no one around."

"Have you looked?"

"I've looked all over."

"Well, switch off the light and sit there in the dark for a while. Just in case."

Freddie said Sure he would, for he was the soul of amiability, and there was an interval of about a quarter of an hour. At the end of that period he said plaintively:

"Hoy."

"Yes?"

"How long does this go on?"

"I don't know. Are you getting awfully bored?"

Freddie admitted that the vigil contained the elements of tedium, and Terry felt discouraged. She was a reasonable girl and quite saw that she could not keep her knight-errant sitting in the dark till daybreak. On the other hand, she could not reveal the true facts. Freddie probably looked on Mrs. Pegler as a second mother and would be deeply offended by the suggestion that she was capable of plotting against girls' welfares with commissaires of police. She was just resigning herself to giving the thing up and allowing Pierre Alexandre Boissonade to go unscathed, when Freddie's voice sounded again at the keyhole, so faintly that she could scarcely hear it. But she caught the word 'Hoy'.

She opened the door an inch.

"What is it?" she whispered.

"There's a guy out there on the balcony."

"Then I was right!"

"Looks that way. Psst!" said Freddie with the hushed conspiratorial intonation of a member of a secret society addressing another member of a secret society, and she closed the door. Plainly the time for action had come, and there must be no more words. A pity, for she would have liked to give her executive a pep talk. Not that Freddie needed pep talks, she reflected. He might be a little on the slow side mentally, but she was safe, she felt, in assuming that he knew the procedure on occasions like this. When the moment arrived for distributing *marrons*, he would be in there swinging and giving of his best. She got into bed again and sat listening tensely.

For what seemed to her an eternity nothing happened. All was silence except for an odd drumming sound which she eventually identified as the beating of her heart. Then abruptly the stillness was shattered and the world became all noise and bustle and activity. A 'Hoy' from Freddie, as might have been expected, opened the proceedings. It was followed by the smashing of glass, the crashing of furniture, the trampling of feet, the heavy breathing of strong men joined in mortal combat and finally by a cry of anguish.

It was from Commissaire Boissonade's lips that this cry had proceeded, and it came from his heart as well, for Freddie's fist, roaming hither and thither in the darkness, had by a lucky chance—or an unlucky one, looking at it from the Commissaire's angle—impinged with considerable force on his right eye. He staggered back, found himself at the open window, reeled on to the balcony, leaped over the rail, and having touched ground vanished into the night. Commissaire Boissonade was brave, but he was not rash. He knew when he had had sufficient.

"Hoy!" said Freddie, speaking once more through the door of the bedroom.

Terry popped her head out.

"My hero!" she said. "Did you kill him?"

"No, he got away."

"Come in and tell me all about it."

She climbed into bed, and Freddie came in, looking a little ruffled but in good shape. Unlike the Commissaire, he had enjoyed the recent exchanges. These last few years he had been troubled more than once by a haunting suspicion that life among the fleshpots had left him out of condition, and it was nice to know that the old pep and vim still lingered.

Yet he was conscious of a certain discontent.

"I ought to have grappled with the fellow and flung him down and sat on his stomach," he said. "Unfortunately I socked him and he flew out of the window. I must be more careful another time."

"You speak as though this sort of thing was going to happen twice nightly for the rest of the summer."

"Well, you never know in these French resort places. Full of jewel thieves."

"You think he was after my jewels?"

"Must have been."

"Thank Heaven you have saved the Trent pearls!"

"Yes, I'm glad of that."

"Also the Trent diamonds, not to mention the Trent sapphires. I really am obliged to you, Butch. Talk about fighting the good fight! You must have had a lot of practice at man-handling your fellow-citizens."

"Oh, well, football, you know. Much the same thing."

"You were wonderful at football, weren't you?"

"I wouldn't say that. I got around, of course, but," said Freddie, laying bare a secret sorrow, "I was never All-American. I wasn't a Snake Todd."

"Who's Snake Todd?"

"You've never heard of Snake Todd?"

"Not that I remember."

"Good God!" said Freddie.

There was a pause, occupied by Freddie in subjecting his hostess to a close scrutiny. Odd, he was thinking, the way women dress up in bed, ribbons and lace and all that. He supposed it was because they thought there might be a fire. The effect, he considered, was undeniably attractive. Eyeing Terry, he tried to imagine Mavis in her place, and going further tried to imagine that that other pillow, the one next to the one which would be hers, was his. The thought drew from him a long, sentimental sigh.

"I don't wonder you're yawning your head off," said Terry. "Go and get to bed."

"Oh, I'm not sleepy," said Freddie, who intended to put in at least a couple more hours looking at the moon. "Say, honestly, do you really mean you never heard of Snake Todd?"

"Never. What is he? A gangster?"

"He was a footballer," said Freddie reverently, "and about the greatest half-back there has ever been in this world. They called him Snake because of the way he used to wriggle through the defence. He was also called Greasy Todd and The Shimmering Spectre. Three years All-American, and his name means nothing to you!"

"Not a thing."

"It's fantastic!" said Freddie, and was on the point of filling in the gaps in this girl's education by describing in detail the eighty-seven-yard run, culminating in a touchdown, which Snake Todd had made in a historic game in 1930, when, as he drew breath to begin, the silence was broken by an odd, furtive, sinister, burglar-like sound, which wiped speech from his lips.

Somebody was turning the handle of the door.

4

He looked at Terry. Terry looked at him. The same thought was in both their minds. Undiscouraged by his experience, Pierre Alexandre Boissonade was in again, this time approaching his objective from a new angle.

Terry was conscious of a reluctant admiration for Pierre
Alexandre Boissonade. She had never met him and did
not like what she had heard of him, but he was unquestionably of the bulldog breed.   Most men who had suffered
as he had done at Freddie's hands, which were like hams,
would have felt that they had had enough.   Their inclina-
tion would have been to give the thing up and call it a day.
But not Pierre Alexandre. His hat was still in the ring.
You can give a Boissonade a *marron*, but you cannot quench
his manly spirit. They make these commissaires, Terry
was thinking, of tough stuff.

But this was no time for idle meditation on the will to win
of the Roville police force, it was a time for action. Waving
a hand in the direction of the bathroom, she wiggled her
eyebrows at Freddie in a meaning manner. What she
was intending to convey was that he should leap into the
bathroom and there remain in hiding till at a suitable
moment, to be selected by himself, he came leaping out
again and began carrying on where he had left off, a
manœuvre which could scarcely fail to make the intruder
feel extremely silly.

The language of the wiggled eyebrow is not always easy
to interpret, and it surprised and gratified Terry to note
that Freddie, whom she had never considered a master-
mind, appeared to find no difficulty in decoding her
message. With an intelligent nod he vanished into the
bathroom with quite a Snake Todd-like agility, and at the
same instant the door opened and Pierre Alexandre Boissonade stood revealed.

Or, rather, what she naturally assumed to be Pierre
Alexandre Boissonade. It was an incorrect diagnosis.
Her visitor, speaking in a confidential whisper, informed
her that he was the *agent d'hôtel*, or, to use a phrase more
familiar to the general public, the house detective. (Pierre
Alexandre himself, now at his residence bathing his eye in a

solution of boracic acid and preparing to put a piece of raw steak on it, would have stated, if questioned, that not even for a king's ransom could he be induced to return to that sinister suite on this night of horror. He had high hopes of some day arresting the Tur-rente woman on some charge that could be made to stick, but—here he attached the steak to his eye—later on would do.)

The house detective was a smallish man with a moustached face and anxious eyes which gave him something of the look of a nervous prawn. He was plainly not at his ease. He had the air of one who was wishing that he had taken up some other walk in life, and that was just how he had been feeling ever since the desk had summoned him to tell him that the occupant of the suite immediately above Terry's had telephoned to say that a murder appeared to be taking place on the floor below, and could someone be sent along to look into the matter. 'Thou art the man,' said the desk, and the house detective, while recognizing that the affair fell into his province, was far from enjoying the situation. The house detective at a hotel like the Splendide does not expect this sort of assignment.

The sight of Terry, not weltering in her blood but seeming at a glance to be perfectly intact, encouraged him.

"Ha!" he said, feeling that things were looking up. "Capital. Excellent."

Terry did not share his enthusiasm. The discovery that he was not Pierre Alexandre Boissonade had relieved her, but she resented this intrusion. No girl likes to have house detectives dropping in when she has gone to bed. It was with considerable asperity that she said:

"What on earth are you doing here?"

The house detective, still speaking in that confidential whisper, explained that a noise, an uproar, a *brouhaha* had been heard.

"Not by me."

"By the occupant of an adjacent suite."

"He——"

"She."

"She must have been dreaming."

"It is possible. But I have been instructed to investigate."

"I don't see that's any reason why you should burst into my bedroom."

The house detective forbore to mention that he had come in that way because he had presumed that assassins were lurking in the main body of the suite. He pursed his lips and shrugged his shoulders, as much as to say that he had his methods.

"Was Mademoiselle asleep?" he asked.

"Yes, fast asleep."

The house detective brightened.

"That is why Mademoiselle did not hear the uproar. One assumes that the *cambrioleur*, entering through the window of the adjoining room, upset some piece of furniture, attracting the notice of the occupant of the suite above. Alarmed, knowing that I would be coming to investigate, he crept in here and concealed himself."

"Where?"

"In the bathroom," said the house detective, inspired.

And a very satisfactory solution of the whole unpleasant affair, he felt. He would, of course, find nobody in the bathroom, but by looking in there he would have done his duty, and would be able to go back and report that investigation had revealed nothing. So thinking, he made for the bathroom door. Few house detectives have ever gone more briskly about a job of work, and few have covered more ground with a backward leap than did he on opening the door of the bathroom and noting contents. It is not too much to say that the sight of Freddie, that very large young man, aged him by several years.

"Cheese!" he exclaimed. It was an ejaculation which he had picked up from a G.I. in Paris, at the end of the war, and he often employed it in moments of great emotion.

He stood staring pallidly. Never having met assassins before, he knew little of their ways, but he had always been given to understand that they can be, when cornered, extremely violent, and his whole soul shrank from violence. He had passed through a most uncomfortable twenty seconds or so when Terry relieved his apprehensions.

"This gentleman is a friend of mine," said Terry.

Just as the scales had fallen from Freddie Carpenter's eyes that night, so did they fall now from the eyes of the house detective. His tenure of office at the Splendide might have left him unfamiliar with the ways of assassins, but what he did not know about gentlemen friends could have been written on a postage stamp. It sometimes seemed to him that a major portion of his adult life had been spent in extracting them from the wrong bedrooms, for there is something in the air of places like Roville that had a most distressing effect on gentlemen friends. His face, as he regarded Freddie, took on its stern official mask.

"I fear Monsieur must leave," he said austerely.

"He was just going," Terry assured him.

"Mademoiselle will appreciate that the situation is irregular."

"Oh, quite."

"For me," said the house detective, suddenly revealing his softer and more sympathetic side, "I would never place obstacles in the way of young love, but the trend of the management's thought is along other lines. Does the gentleman understand French?"

"Not a word."

"Then perhaps Mademoiselle would have the kindness to explain to him that it is necessary for him to return to his own apartment. And quick (*au trot*)," said the house detective.

"I'll tell him."

"Thank you, mademoiselle," said the house detective, and withdrew, clicking his tongue.

"What was all that?" asked Freddie. "I wish I understood this ghastly language."

Terry interpreted.

"He was saying you will have to tear yourself away. I'm afraid he put an unpleasant construction on your being in my bathroom at this advanced hour in blue pyjamas."

A crimson blush spread itself over Freddie's face, a blush partly of embarrassment but principally of wrath. The most chivalrous of young men, his blood boiled freely when house detectives spoke lightly of a woman's name.

"Of all the nerve! I'll go and knock his block off."

"Don't blame him. He's French. Frenchmen always think the worst."

"Then I'm glad I'm American."

"Me, too. Oh, say can you see by the dawn's early light what——"

"What?"

"That's what I'm saying . . . what? What comes after that?"

"I couldn't tell you. I generally hum from there on."

"So do I. As the song says, No one knows the words but the Argentines and the Portugese and the Greeks. Yes, you must go, Butch, I fear. Thanks ever so much for dropping in. You were simply wonderful."

"Oh, no."

"But I can't send you out into the night without a drink. You would like one, wouldn't you, after all your exertions?"

"I could do with a drink."

"Then let's go into the other room. Golly!" said Terry, as she switched the light on and surveyed the battlefield. "What a mess! Which of you was it upset the lamp?"

"I think we split it about fifty-fifty. I'll tidy up, shall I?"

"Do. I'll be getting the refreshments."

Freddie was a quick worker. When Terry returned with whisky and sandwiches on a tray, he had done his task so well that not a trace of the recent grim struggle remained. As Terry said, you would never know that there had been a burglar. They sat down, and Freddie applied himself to his glass.

"This is cosy," he said, lowering it.

"Very cosy. Have a sandwich."

"Thanks. You know," said Freddie, returning to the subject uppermost in his thoughts, "you amazed me when you said you had never heard of Snake Todd."

"I'm not very well up in football. I've only seen one game in my life."

"Good God!"

"And that was enough. It all seemed so silly."

"*Silly!*"

"That's how it struck me."

"What was there silly about it?"

"Well, when a group of young men spend the afternoon going off into a corner and putting their heads together with their behinds sticking up . . ."

"The huddle." Freddie spoke stiffly. "You can't play football without huddling."

"I still say it's silly."

A stunned silence fell upon Freddie. The whole atmosphere of the agreeable *tête-à-tête* had been ruined for him. It had been bad enough to learn that this girl had not heard of Snake Todd, but that she could consider the huddle silly . . . He shivered. It is never nice for a devout man to hear blasphemy from the lips of youth and beauty.

"They would have been far better employed," said Terry, summing up, "staying at home and reading a good book."

Freddie was not listening. His mind had floated back
to the moment at the dinner table when with the aid of
twenty-two lumps of sugar he had demonstrated to Mavis
Todd a complicated play which had been presented to his
notice at last year's Army-Navy game. How different,
how infinitely more fitting her attitude had been. He
could still see the rapt interest in her eyes as the lump of
sugar that was carrying the ball had threaded its way
through the opposition lumps of sugar and scored a touchdown while thousands cheered.

"Or doing crossword puzzles," said Terry. "Or getting
on with their knitting. Or——"

She broke off with a gulp, and a similar gulp proceeded
from Freddie. He shot out of his chair and stood looking
like a statue of himself subscribed for and presented to the
community by a few warm friends and admirers. For
from outside in the passage there had sounded a sudden
burst of laughter, and the door was opening. The next
moment, Kate came in, followed by Old Nick, who was
followed by a little dried-up man in rimless pince-nez with
English Civil Servant written all over him.

5

Kate, contrary to her expectations, had had a delightful
evening. There had been an awkward moment at the outset when she had informed her host of Terry's headache,
for the news seemed to upset Mrs. Pegler, but after that no
function could have been pleasanter. Seated next to Old
Nick, she had found him at his most charming, not a suggestion in his manner that there lingered in his mind
memories of their last meeting, and had gradually sur-
rendered to his spell. Old Nick could be fascinating when
he exerted himself, and it had seemed to him very necessary

that he should exert himself to conciliate a woman who, if disposed, could do him a great deal of harm in Roville. By the time they set out on the homeward journey in the car of Sir Percy Bunt of the English Civil Service they were virtually old friends, and it was at an amusing anecdote of his that she had just been laughing so heartily.

Then she saw Freddie, and her laughter died away with a gurgling sound like bath water going down a waste pipe. She stood for a frozen instant taking in his pyjamas, his tousled hair and his expression of obvious guilt, then turned her gaze on Terry, and it was the gaze of one who might have been Mrs. Grundy's twin sister. Incapable of speech, she jerked her head silently at her bedroom door and moved toward it. Terry followed her meekly. The door closed behind them.

The sight of Freddie had occasioned Old Nick, too, a certain surprise. But he had had long experience in passing off delicate situations.

"Ah, Butch," he said. "Still up and about? I wonder if you know Sir Percy Bunt? Sir Percy Bunt, Mr. Carpenter."

"How do you do?"

"Mr. Carpenter owns the majority of the stock in Fizzo, which you probably drink."

"Fizzo? Oh, rather," said Sir Percy, giving Freddie a respectful look that seemed to say that he was one of the fans. "I take it with a little whisky at night. My wife prefers it with a little lemon. Talking of wives, I hope we didn't drive your good lady away, barging in like this."

"What good lady?" asked Freddie, never very quick at the uptake.

"Your wife," said Sir Percy, indicating the bedroom door.

"Oh, we aren't married," said Freddie, and Sir Percy, jumping, drew in his breath with a sharp hiss. He knew that French seashore resorts were lax and licentious, but he had not supposed them to be as lax and licentious as this. His manner was so austere that even Freddie noticed it and hastened to put things right by telling the story of the nocturnal marauder.

It was not a success. As the tale proceeded, he became oppressed by the feeling that his audience was finding it thin. It sounded thin to himself.

"That's how it was," he concluded, his voice trailing off in a mumble so full of hangdog guilt that Sir Percy's worst suspicions were confirmed.

"I see. Well, I think I will be saying good night," said Sir Percy in accents that sounded like ice tinkling in a tumbler, and went out stiffly. The look he cast at Freddie as he turned in the doorway could hardly have been more censorious if the latter had been a veiled adventuress diffusing a strange exotic scent whom he had discovered in the act of stealing secret treaties from the drawer of his desk in Whitehall. It smote Freddie like a blow, and he was still reeling under it when he became aware that Old Nick was addressing him.

"Well, really, Butch!" said Old Nick.

"Eh?"

"Could you not have thought up something better than that?"

"Eh?"

"Burglars... Struggles in the dark... Tut, tut!"

"But I did struggle with a burglar in the dark."

"H'm."

"I socked him, and he got away."

"H'm."

"I wish you wouldn't keep saying 'H'm'. Why do you say 'H'm'?"

"I say 'H'm', my boy, because I find your explanation hard to believe. I see no signs of a struggle."

"I tidied up."

"H'm."

"There you go again. I tell you that's what *happened*."

"H'm."

"Oh, stop it!"

"I wish I could. I mean," said Old Nick gravely, "stop Sir Percy Bunt telling the story which he will unquestionably spread all over Roville, starting tomorrow. The full story of what he saw here tonight."

Freddie leaped like a salmon in the spawning season.

"He wouldn't do that?"

"He will probably dine out on the thing for weeks."

"Oh, golly!" Freddie buried his face in his hands. He had not felt so shattered since the afternoon when, dying for dear old Princeton, he had received on his stomach the full impact of a platoon of human mastodons who were dying for dear old Yale. "Oh, gosh!" he moaned. "Why didn't I scram when that dick told me to?"

"Who is this Richard of whom you speak?"

"The house dick. The house detective. He was in here just now."

Old Nick drew his breath in sharply.

"In here? The *agent d'hôtel* saw you *too?* In this room?"

"In the bathroom, as a matter of fact."

"In the bathroom? Well," said Old Nick, having drawn another sharp breath, "this settles it. There is only one thing to be done, only one course you can pursue. You must immediately publish the announcement of your engagement to Miss Trent."

"What!"

"Did I not," said Old Nick, and his manner was cold, "speak distinctly?"

"But I want to marry somebody else."

"It is not what you want that matters, my boy. There is such a thing as doing one's duty," said Old Nick, speaking of course from hearsay. "You cannot compromise a lady and behave as if nothing had happened. The breath of scandal . . ."

"But, darn it——"

"As a man of honour, you have no alternative."

Freddie sat plunged in thought, and Old Nick watched him as he had so often watched the roulette ball as it spun around the board. So much that was vital depended on this young man's decision . . . his loved son's release from a penniless girl . . . the securing by way of compensation for this girl, for whom from the first he had felt a paternal fondness, of a husband whose riches made the mind reel.

An aeon passed. Freddie looked up. His face was twisted.

"Okay," he said.

"Splendid fellow," said Old Nick, and went off to telephone to the Paris *New York Herald-Tribune*.

He had scarcely left when Terry came out of Kate's bedroom. She was looking a little battered, as if she had passed through some stern and testing ordeal, as indeed she had. Always eloquent on the occasions when her younger sisters' behaviour seemed to her to call for rebuke, Kate tonight had touched new high levels of achievement.

"Good heavens, Butch," said Terry. "You still here? I thought you had gone ages ago."

"No, I stuck around. I was talking to old Maufringnooze. Listen."

"I'm listening."

"I just wanted to say it's all right."

"I'm glad you think so. Try selling that thought to Kate."

"I mean about us. I'd like to marry you, if you think well of the idea."

"Why, Butch!"

"Will you marry me?"

"No."

"Old Maufringnooze advises it."

"Old Maufringnooze can mind his own darned business."

"He talked about the breath of scandal."

"Let it breathe. Don't think I don't appreciate your very chivalrous offer, Butch, but you needn't worry about me. Between ourselves, if you think you can keep a secret, I am expecting shortly to get married elsewhere."

"You don't say!"

"That's the way things seem to point."

"You mean you love somebody else?"

"That's right."

Illumination came to Freddie.

"Jeff?"

"Right again."

Freddie beamed.

"Well, this is fine. He's a great guy."

"That's how he strikes me."

"French, mind you," said Freddie, for one must always look at every side of a thing, even the dark side. "You can't get away from that. Still, his mother was American."

"Then I think we may safely pass him, don't you?" said Terry. "Okay, Butch, run along and get some sleep, and thanks for a very pleasant visit. Give my love to Snake Todd."

It was at this moment that Kate came out of her room, looking like Mrs. Siddons as Lady Macbeth. At the sight of Freddie a sheet of flame shot from her eyes, and Freddie, getting it squarely, recoiled to the french window. With a mumbled something which might have been a 'Good night' he backed on to the balcony, stood silhouetted for an instant against the summer sky, then vanished with the agility of a cat leaving a strange alley. Intrepid when faced by human mastodons, he found himself unequal to exchanging ideas with Kate. She always affected him as she affected Henry Weems of the firm of Kelly, Dubinsky, Wix, Weems and Bassinger.

"Well, really!" said Kate.

"You were surprised to find him still here?" said Terry. "It's all right. He lingered on to ask me to marry him."

"Oh!" It would be too much to say that Kate's steely front softened, but she seemed to be experiencing a grudging relief. "Yes, I suppose it's the best way out of an appalling situation."

"But I declined the gentleman's offer."

"What!"

"I like Freddie Carpenter very very much, but I'm not going to marry him."

Kate stared.

"Are you serious?"

"Quite."

"You can't be. Terry, I sometimes think you are insane. Don't you realize . . ."

"Oh, stop it, Kate! It's no use talking."

"It never is with you."

Quick of temper, Terry was always quickly remorseful.

"I'm sorry, darling. I didn't mean to bite your head off. I suppose all tonight's excitement has made me jumpy."

"*And rude*. I shall go to bed. Oh," said Kate, pausing and opening her bag, "I was forgetting. They gave me this note for you downstairs when I was getting my key. Good night," she said, and went into her room, slamming the door.

6

Kate's enjoyment of Mrs. Pegler's dinner had been, as has been said, considerable, but if there is a drawback to

dinners where a Marquis de Maufringneuse et Valerie-
Moberanne orders the food and wine regardless of expense it
is that those who participate in them are apt, when they get
home, to feel a little fevered and in urgent need of bicarbonate of soda. Kate did. It was not long after she made
her impressive exit that she returned to the sitting-room,
looking pale and proud.

"I want some bicarbonate of soda," she said haughtily.

Terry did not answer. She was at the table writing.

"I want," repeated Kate, "some bicarbonate of soda."

Terry turned. Her face was white and her eyes sombre.

"There's some in my bathroom."

"Thank you."

There was a pause.

"Aren't you ever going to bed?" said Kate.

"As soon as I've finished this letter," said Terry, resuming work on it.

"To whom are you writing?" asked Kate, still haughty,
but inquisitive.

"To Freddie Carpenter. If you go out before I do tomorrow, you might leave it at the desk. It's just a line to
say that I will marry him."

"What! Then you feel now that I was right?"

"You're always right. It's uncanny. You were so right
about Jeff. You said I should get a polite letter from him
saying that he had unfortunately been called away. Well,
there it is on that table over there. You can read it if you
like," said Terry, and, getting up, flung herself sobbing on
the sofa.

"Oh, honey!" cried Kate, no longer the stern elder
sister, and ran to her and rocked her in her arms.

CHAPTER EIGHT

THE Clutterbuck lunch was an unqualified success, going like a breeze from the opening martini. It was one of those lunches which mark epochs and remain photographically lined on the tablets of the mind when a yesterday has faded from its page.

It had occasionally happened, for these moods of despondency come to all of us from time to time, that Jeff, viewing the human race, had found himself doing so with concern, regretting that he belonged to it and asking himself if Man could really be Nature's last word. German soldiers had often set his mind working along these lines, and so had the concierge at his lodgings in the Rue Jacob. But today, seated opposite Russell Clutterbuck at the luncheon table, he saw how wrong he had been to harbour such thoughts. The human race was all right. Any race that could produce a Russell Clutterbuck was entitled to slap itself on the chest and go strutting about with its thumbs in the armholes of its waistcoat and its hat on the side of its head.

Physically, it is true, this splendid specimen of humanity fell somewhat short of the ideal. In the outer crust of Russell Clutterbuck, as Jeff would have been the first to admit, there was little or nothing to provoke excited cheering from the populace. Unlike most publishers, who tend to become lean and haggard from mixing with authors, he bulged opulently in all directions and with his round face, round eyes and round spectacles looked like an owl which has been doing itself too well on the field-mice.

What set him on a pinnacle above his fellow-men was his conversation.

It was not immediately that his gifts in this direction had impressed themselves on Jeff, for over the cocktails he had spoken only of the gratification he felt at being in Paris without his wife. Mrs. Clutterbuck, he said, though the best little woman in the world, did not understand him. He found it impossible to drive it into her nut that a busy brain-worker, if he hopes to escape ulcers, has to have occasional interludes in his life of toil when he can relax and go around seeing the sights and having broadening experiences. His sentiments were almost exactly those which Jeff had heard expressed on the previous night by Chester Todd.

Through the early stages of the substantial meal which he had ordered—for he made it plain from the beginning that he was in no sense on a diet—he continued to touch upon this theme, paying a handsome tribute to the kindly Providence which had caused the moon of his delight to contract mumps on the eve of departure, but with the porterhouse steak and fried potatoes he got down to business, and it was then that the full charm of the man's personality was brought home to Jeff.

"That book of yours," said Russell Clutterbuck, attacking his steak with tooth and claw. "It surprised me. Where did you learn to write English that way? Nobody would think you were French."

"My mother was American. I've been bilingual all my life."

"And you write about America as if you'd been there."

"I have. My father married again and I didn't get on very well with my stepmother, so I cleared off and went to America. I was there several years, doing various jobs. I was on the waterfront for a time, and I worked on a dude ranch and went prospecting with a friend of mine in the

Mojave desert and . . . oh, lots of things. When the war broke out, I was a waiter at a New York hotel."

"Which hotel was that?"

"The Burbage."

"I've lunched there. Food good, but portions too small. So you came back to shed your blood for France?"

"That was the idea. As it happened, I didn't shed much. But it was always there, if wanted."

"You weren't in this what they call the Macky?"

"Yes, I was in the Maquis."

"Have a bad time?"

"It was tough in spots."

"Didn't get much to eat, I imagine?"

"Not much."

"I can understand how you must have felt. I've been through the same sort of thing myself. I've a country house at a place called Bensonburg on Long Island, and one Sunday, just as we were having our cocktails before lunch, in comes the butler and says the cook's compliments and the Great Dane belonging to some people down the road came into the kitchen while her back was turned and went off with the roast of lamb. Nothing to be done. Nearest butcher's six miles away in Westhampton, and shut of course on a Sunday. Had to fall back on eggs. I had five or six with bacon, followed by buckwheat cakes and maple syrup, and after that I did the best I could with cheese. I got by, but I wouldn't care to have to go through a thing like that again. Garsong, encore de fried potatoes," said Russell Clutterbuck. "Well, that's very interesting what you say about being in the Macky. Good stuff for the blurb on the jacket."

Jeff choked. He stared at his host much as one supposes M. Letondu must have stared on first seeing the shining figure which had recommended hitting M. de La Hourmerie on the head with a hatchet.

"Would you mind saying that again?" he said.

"You mean about the fried potatoes?"

"No, about the blurb on the jacket. You spoke of the blurb on the jacket."

"That's right."

"Then there's going to be a jacket?"

"Got to have a jacket."

"I mean, you're going to publish my book?"

"Sure," said Russell Clutterbuck, and looked more like a shining figure than anything Jeff had ever seen. "It's just the kind of book I like. It's gay. It's amusing. It's riskay but not too riskay. Reminded me a little of Evelyn Waugh. And it's about human beings like you meet on the train every morning coming in from Great Neck and not a bunch of blasted sharecroppers getting all persecuted down in Alabama or somewhere. If you knew," said Russell Clutterbuck, helping himself bitterly to fried potatoes, "how many novels about persecuted sharecroppers I have to read every year, you'd shudder."

"They crop up, these croppers?"

"You can't stop 'em. And if it isn't sharecroppers, it's crippled children. Look," said Russell Clutterbuck, shovelling fried potatoes into himself like a stevedore loading a grain ship. "Here's the plot of the one I read coming over on the plane. There's this illegitimate crippled child with brutal stepfather. Stepfather whales the tar out of the unfortunate little bastard for sixteen pages with a horse whip and then hauls off and murders his mother. Child's mother, I mean, not stepfather's mother. Child goes mad and dies in a cornfield. Stepfather hangs himself, father of child shoots himself. How many corpses is that?"

"Four, I make it."

"I should have said more, but maybe you're right. And there's a girl who gets her face burned up in a fire and a child—not the first child, another child, small-part child—

who's run over by a sightseeing bus and loses both legs. Just to think of it takes my appetite away," said Russell Clutterbuck, cleaving his steak as Sir Galahad with his good sword clove the casques of men. "You can imagine what a relief this thing of yours was. By the way, you sent it to me direct, with that letter from Brice, so I take it you don't have an agent? Fine," he said, reassured on this point, and spoke his mind about agents for a while, comparing them unfavourably to the late Jesse James and telling a rather long story about one of them whose ethical standards would, unless he was much mistaken, have excited shocked comment in the fo'c'sle of a pirate ship. "Then we can go ahead and handle the thing for you. You've probably been thinking that we've taken our time letting you know what we felt about it. That's because I was seeing people."

"Seeing people?"

"The magazines and the movies and the Pocket Book people. They're interested. Yessir, they're sitting up and taking notice. When I told them we expected to sell a hundred thousand——"

The Ritz grillroom did a Nijinsky leap before Jeff's eyes. When it had returned to terra firma, he said:

"You told them you were expecting to sell a hundred thousand copies?"

"We always tell them we're expecting to sell a hundred thousand copies," said Russell Clutterbuck, letting him in on one of the secrets of the publishing trade.

2

With mutual expressions of goodwill Jeff parted from his publisher at seven o'clock on the following morning. It was not that their very agreeable luncheon had extended itself until then, but Mr. Clutterbuck had insisted on his company at dinner and after that on an all-night tour of Montmartre and other pleasure centres which had culminated in a refreshing bowl of onion soup down at the Markets. It was past ten when Jeff alighted from Freddie Carpenter's Cadillac and went to his room to get a much-needed sleep.

Shortly after he had done so, Kate came out of the hotel. She had been conscious on rising of a slight headache, for though last night's bicarbonate of soda had done much it had not done everything, and she was hoping that a breath of sea air would turn the scale. Taking the note to Freddie Carpenter, to leave it at the desk, she set forth in her sensible shoes along the Promenade des Anglais.

It was a beautiful morning of gentle breezes and golden sunshine, and Roville was at its gayest. Stout gentlemen frisked in the shallow water, other stout gentlemen lay on the sands, covered with oil, turning themselves a revolting brown. The excellent weather conditions effected a speedy cure. When she returned an hour later, she was looking better and feeling brighter. She heard Terry moving about in her room and hailed her cheerily.

"Terry."

"Yes?"

"I gave your note to the man at the desk. Mr. Carpenter won't get it till after lunch. He went out early to play golf." She came to the open door of Terry's room and stared in, amazed. "What on earth are you doing?" she asked.

"Packing," said Terry shortly.

"Packing?"

"We're going home on the next plane. At least, I am." Kate sniffed.

"Oh, I'll come too, if that's what you mean, and only too glad to. I've seen all of Europe I want. You can have Europe. But isn't this rather sudden?"

"I suppose so," said Terry, and as Kate saw the misery in her face, her iron front came very near to melting. But she was a woman who went in for strength of character and did not believe in emotional scenes. Already she was more than a little ashamed of her lapse into weakness of the previous night, feeling that what she described to herself as 'all that sort of nonsense' ought to be discouraged. So now she simply said:

"How about Mr. Carpenter?"

"What about him?"

"Won't he think this sudden departure odd?"

"Not after he has read the note I've just written him."

"You've written him another note?"

"Yes. I'm going to leave it at the desk when I go to get the tickets."

Another sniff escaped Kate.

"The way you write notes, you might be a Foreign Office. What did you tell him?"

"Just that I'm not going to marry him. I've been thinking it over, and I realize that I can't go through with it."

Kate sniffed for the third time. This was one of the things—one of the many—with which she had, as she often put it, no patience. If there was one type of person who exasperated her more than most types of person, it was the type of person who did not know his or her mind. When she herself came to a decision, it stayed come to.

"I give you up," she said, sniffing a fourth and final sniff. "Last night he asked you to marry him and you said you wouldn't. Then you wrote saying you would. And now you have written saying you won't. I'm sorry for that young man. He will be wondering if he's standing on his head or his heels."

3

Another young man who was in a rather similar condition was Chester Todd. At about the hour of one he was sitting on the terrace outside the Casino Municipale feeling dazed and fragile. He was never quite himself after one of his evenings out, and he had now had two evenings out in succession, for on the previous night he had run into some friends from America with views on revelry as spacious as his own. At this moment he was quite definitely below par, and the thought that his Aunt Hermione was seated at his side and shortly about to lunch with him did nothing to raise his spirits. He was wondering what madness had led him to attempt to give lunch to an aunt on what he should have foreseen would have been one of those mornings calling for complete solitude and perfect quiet.

Mrs. Pegler, too, was not at her brightest. She had just been in telephonic communication with Commissaire Boissonade—she had been unable to reach him on the previous day, an eye injury confining him to his home—and had learned from him of the fiasco of the night before last. The Commissaire had been rather cross on the telephone.

Conversation, accordingly, had flagged, and it was after a silence of some minutes that Chester suddenly uttered an exclamation.

"Gosh!" he said, and with a quick hand succeeded in stopping his head from coming off. "That's a pretty girl!"

Terry was the girl to whom he alluded. To purchase reservations on the transatlantic plane, it is necessary, if you are in Roville, to go to the ticket office in the lobby of the Casino Municipale, and to reach this office you have to cross the terrace. Mrs. Pegler, following her nephew's gaze, inspected her coldly.

"If," she said aloofly, "you admire that chocolate-box type of prettiness."

"Chocolate-box nothing!" said Chester, outraged by the implication that he was not a connoisseur of female comeliness. "She's a pippin. The odd thing is, I've an idea I've seen her before somewhere. I wonder who she is."

"Her name is Trent."

"Oh, you know her?"

"We are acquainted. Frederick met her at St. Rocque."

"I met a girl called Trent at St. Rocque."

"Oh?"

"She and Jane and Freddie and I dined together one night. Some relation, perhaps?"

"I believe Miss Trent has no relations except a sister in America."

"Well, it's very odd. I have a distinct recollection of having seen that girl before. But where?"

"Does it matter?"

"No, I suppose it doesn't," said Chester, and the little spurt of conversation died away. Mrs. Pegler resumed her sombre thoughts of Pierre Alexandre Boissonade, now classified in her mind as an incompetent bungler whom she should never have trusted with a mission calling for shrewdness, initiative and know-how, and Chester, slumped in his seat, sat listening to the steam-riveting in progress inside his head and wondering how he was to get through this ghastly lunch alone and unaided. His emotions when a few minutes later he saw his sister Mavis approaching, followed by Freddie Carpenter, resembled those of the shipwrecked mariner who sights a sail. He was one of Freddie's warmest admirers, and would have been glad of his company at any time, but now the stalwart youth seemed to him sent from heaven. He greeted him with a warmth that threatened once again to detach his head from the parent spine.

"Hi, Butch!" he cried.

"Hi," said Freddie.

"Have a good game?"

"Fine."

"I picked your mail up at the hotel."

"Oh, thanks."

"I had an idea you would be looking in here. You're just in time for lunch."

"Mavis and I thought of lunching at the Miramar."

"You aren't lunching at any by golly Miramars," said Chester firmly. He intended to avoid being closeted alone with his Aunt Hermione even if it involved stunning Freddie with a chair and dragging him into the Casino restaurant by the scruff of his neck. "You're lunching here with us."

"Well, if you say so," said Freddie, always amiable. "Okay with you, darl— I mean Mavis?"

"Yes, Freddie," said Mavis, rationing herself strictly, as was her habit in the matter of words, and they went in.

It was not long after they had seated themselves at the table that Chester became conscious of a sense of disappointment and frustration. He had been so confident that the addition of Freddie to the party would have stepped up the volume of small talk, for Freddie, fresh from a round of golf, could usually be relied on for some pretty lively stuff about what he had done at the long eleventh or the short fourth or whatever hole it might be. Today, however, he was strangely silent, and this threw on the invalid host a considerably heavier burden of social effort than he could have wished. He had hoped to be able to lean back in his chair and play a thinking part, letting the world go by.

And then suddenly everything brightened. Mrs. Pegler, coming to life, remarked what a pity it was that people were in such a rush these days, dashing about everywhere and declining to stay put. She instanced a friend of hers, Sir Percy Bunt of the British Civil Service. She had tried to persuade him to stay on in Roville for the remainder of his leave from the Foreign Office, but no, he would insist on going on with this motor tour of his. Some nonsense about wanting to see France.

It was at this point that Freddie, who had been crumbling bread, started as if electrified.

"Has that Bunt guy left?"

"He went yesterday after breakfast."

"He . . ." Freddie coughed in rather a strangled way. "He didn't . . . er . . . *say* anything, did he?"

"I don't understand you."

"About me, I mean—I just wondered if he had mentioned me."

"Why should he mention you?"

"Oh, no special reason."

"He was only here one day, and I don't think you met him. I'm surprised that you have heard of him."

"Oh, everybody's heard of Sir Percy Bunt," said Freddie heartily, and became a changed man, starting immediately to relate in detail the happy results which had ensued when—on the dog-leg seventh—he had decided to try a more open stance.

All this took place over the coffee at the end of the meal, and with everything now going with such a swing Chester, though aware that a host should not be the first to make a move, felt justified in stretching a point and leaving his guests to their merrymaking. He got up, saying that he wanted to go and buy a Paris *New York Herald-Tribune*, to see what they had said about his wife Jane's violin recital.

It was almost immediately after he had taken his head carefully out into the Roville sunshine that Freddie, turning almost as red as his hair, gave another of his strangled coughs.

"Er, Mrs. Pegler," he said.

He cast an agonized glance at Mavis, as if in the hope of receiving support, but Mavis, true to her Trappist vows, preserved her customary silence.

"Er, Mrs. Pegler," said Freddie, reluctantly resigning himself to the unpleasant task of being the principal after-luncheon speaker. That quiet of Mavis's which he so admired cut, he reflected, both ways. He could have done just now with more garrulity. "Er, Mrs. Pegler, there's something I would like to mention, if you could spare me a moment."

"Yes, Frederick?"

With the aid of a sip of brandy, Freddie marshalled his thoughts.

"I don't know if you know the fifteenth hole here?"

"I do not play golf."

"Oh? Well, it's rather a tricky hole. Simple enough if you keep your drive straight, but plenty of trouble if you slice, because there's a lot of undergrowth to the right to catch a sliced shot. I had the honour, and I got off a nice one down the middle, possibly—I think probably—because of this open stance I was speaking of. Mavis, however, when it came to her turn to perform, sliced rather badly and went into this undergrowth I was speaking of. So we started to look for her ball together, and what with one thing and another, while in this undergrowth I was speaking of, we got into conversation about this and that and finally . . . Under a pine tree, was it not?"

"Yes, Freddie," said Mavis.

"Until finally, under this pine tree I was speaking of," proceeded Freddie, blushfully delivering the punch line, "I asked her to be my wife, and, to cut a long story short, she said she would."

He paused. It was an apprehensive pause. Essentially modest, he felt dubious about the view an aunt might take of her niece's bethrothal to a man who, though reasonably competent on the football field, had never— let's face it—made the All-American.   It was with a surge of relief and joy that he observed that Mrs. Pegler, who might quite well have been staring coldly at him through a lorgnette, was wreathed in smiles.

"Why, Frederick!" said Mrs. Pegler.

"I hope you aren't sore."

"Sore!"

"There's this, of course, to bear in mind," said Freddie, pointing out the silver lining.   "You may be losing a niece—in fact, you are losing a niece—but you are gaining a nephew."

"And just the nephew I would like to gain."

"You don't mean that?"

"Of course I do."

"Well, that's fine. That's splendid. That's terrific. I was rather wondering if you might not think that Mavis, with an uncle like Snake Todd, had more or less thrown herself away, as it were.   I'm not much of a fellow."

"You're a splendid fellow, Frederick dear, and I know you will be very, very happy, Mavis."

"Yes, Auntie," said Mavis.

"I've never been more delighted in my life," said Mrs. Pegler.   She kissed Freddie, who had been afraid of this but told himself with the splendid Carpenter fortitude that at such a time one has to take the rough with the smooth. "I had been hoping and hoping that this would happen." A keen, predatory look came into her face.   "I shall go right off and play at the big table," she said.   "I feel this is my lucky day.   You won't mind me leaving you?"

"No, Auntie," said Mavis.

"Not a bit," said Freddie, and he had seldom spoken straighter from the heart.   "You go right ahead and skin those dagoes to the bone."

In order to skin to the bone the dagoes at the big table at
the Roville—or any other—Casino, it is necessary to supply
yourself with the sinews of war. Mrs. Pegler's first move,
accordingly, was to proceed to the *caisse* and cash a cheque
for five hundred thousand francs. And she had just
stuffed the bundle of notes into her bag, when she was aware
of her nephew Chester at her elbow.

"Oh, Chester!" she said. "Such wonderful news.
Mavis is engaged."

"No, really?" said Chester, interested. "What a coincidence. So is Freddie."

"Well, of course."

This annoyed Chester. His head was still paining him.

"I don't know why you say 'Of course'. I consider
it a most remarkable coincidence that he and Mavis should
have got engaged simultaneously like this. Doesn't often
happen, that sort of thing. Who's the man?"

Mrs. Pegler, weighing this against that, came to the
conclusion that this was one of her nephew's jokes. She did
not think it a very good joke, but she chuckled merrily.
She shared the view of the sage who said that we ought to
laugh at the jokes which are not funny, because the funny
ones can look after themselves.

"You are silly, Chester. Frederick, of course."

Chester shook his head, a foolish thing to do, for it encouraged an unseen hand to drive a red-hot spike into it.

"No, there," he said, when the agony had abated, "I
take issue with you. There, if you don't mind me saying so,
you're talking through the back of your. neck. The girl
Freddie's engaged to is that Miss Trent we saw coming
across the terrace before lunch. It's in the paper," said
Chester, exhibiting the *Herald-Tribune* and indicating with a
pointing finger an item on the front page. "Look for
yourself."

CHAPTER NINE

THERE are some shocks so devastating that they afflict the recipient with a sort of catalepsy, depriving him or her of the power of speech and movement. For a full minute after her nephew had wandered away in the dreamy manner habitual with young men suffering from hangovers she stood as if, like Lot's wife, she had been turned into a pillar of salt. Then, recovering the use of her limbs, she went off to talk things over with Freddie.

On the way to the restaurant she met Mavis. The sight of the unfortunate girl, so plainly happy, so obviously not in touch with current developments, might have extorted her pity, had she been in a frame of mind to have pity extorted from her. As it was, she merely panted a little.

"Where is Frederick?" she asked, in a hollow voice. "Is he in the restaurant?"

"No, Auntie," said Mavis, and becoming—for her—quite chatty, explained that she, having a letter to write, was returning to the hotel for a few minutes, while her betrothed had sought the seclusion of the bar, always quiet at this time of day, in order to skim through his mail.

He had just finished skimming through it when Mrs. Pegler found him, and as the last item of his reading matter had been the first of Terry's two notes, she found him in poor shape. He was sprawled bonelessly in a chair at the far end of the room, gazing before him with what are usually described as unseeing eyes. When Mrs. Pegler, looming up at the table, took the chair beside him, he found it hard to focus her through the murky mist which was interfering with his powers of vision.

"Well, Frederick," said Mrs. Pegler, directing at him a look which might have come straight from a flame-thrower, "what is all this? What does it mean? What have you to say? I should be glad of an explanation."

His mind a little clearer now, Freddie was able to appreciate the necessity of making something in the nature of an explanation to this understandably incandescent aunt, and, going further, he realized that such an explanation would have to be a categorical one. But, as so often happens with categorical explanations, the difficulty was to know where to begin.

"You mean about Terry Trent?" he said.

"I do," said Mrs. Pegler.

"She says she's going to marry me."

"So I understand."

"Yup," said Freddie, "she says she's going to marry me, and it's come as quite a surprise, because when I asked her if she would, she said she wouldn't."

Mrs. Pegler told herself that she must be calm . . . calm. All the woman in her called imperiously to her to beat this man into a jelly with her bag, but she restrained the generous impulse. To put temptation out of her way, she placed the bag on the floor.

"You admit then that you asked her to marry you?"

"Oh, yes, I asked her all right."

"Are you in the habit of proposing marriage right and left to every girl you meet?"

"Good heavens, no. But this was rather a special occasion. You see——"

"You are wrong. I do not see."

"Well, it was like this."

The ability to tell a story clearly and well is not given to all, and Freddie was one of those who had been overlooked in the distribution. He rambled and was obscure, and at the conclusion of his recital of the events of that fateful night Mrs. Pegler found herself as far as ever from grasping what Henry Weems, of the firm of Kelly, Dubinsky, Wix, Weems and Bassinger, would have called the *minutiae*.

"I cannot make head or tail of what you are saying," she said.

"Not clear?"

"Clear!" said Mrs. Pegler, snorting emotionally. "I don't understand a word of it. Why should you have asked this girl to marry you?"

"Old Maufringnooze advised it."

Mrs. Pegler started like a harpooned whale. Her aspect was that of one who sees all. How it had come about she did not know . . . the details would have to be filled in later . . . but somehow, in some way, she was convinced that her late husband's had been the directing hand behind this dreadful thing that had shaken her to her foundations. She saw it as the culmination of a Machiavellian plot between him and the Trent girl, and a sigh shook her. She was thinking how often during the years she had spent with Nicolas Jules St. Xavier Auguste, Marquis de Maufringneuse et Valerie-Moberanne, the most admirable opportunities had presented themselves of dropping something hard and heavy on his head from an upstairs landing, and those opportunities she had wantonly neglected. Of all sad words of tongue or pen the saddest are these, 'It might have been.'

"So he was there?" she said, and her teeth snapped together with a little clicking sound. She had not actually gnashed them, but she had come very close to it.

"Sure," said Freddie. "Didn't I tell you that? It's the whole point of the thing. He came in with the Bunt guy, and after the Bunt guy had gone, he talked a blue streak about the breath of scandal and how the only

honourable thing I could do was to ask Terry to marry me.
I can't remember if he said 'Noblesse oblige', but one could
see that that was what he was driving at. And I got his
point, mind you. I mean, there I was, alone with Terry
in my pyjamas. . . ."

"Your *pyjamas*?"

"Yup. You see, I had more or less retired for the night
when she called me over. So, as I was saying, I asked
her to marry me, and she gave me the brusheroo, and I,
thinking I had the green light, proposed to Mavis in that
undergrowth I was speaking of. And now comes a note
from her saying 'Ignore the brusheroo. The wedding is
on'. It's a mix-up," said Freddie, wagging his scarlet
head, "and there's no use trying to pretend it's not." A
point which he had overlooked, and was surprised that he
had overlooked, occurred to him. "But how did you know
about it?" he asked.

"It's in the paper."

"In the *paper*?"

"You will find the announcement of your engagement
to Miss Trent in today's *Paris Herald-Tribune*."

"Gosh!"

"How it got there I cannot imagine."

Freddie uttered a cry.

"I can. Old Maufringnooze must have phoned them
after he left me. Golly! What am I going to do?"

"You intend to marry Mavis?"

"Good heavens, yes. She's the only girl I've ever met
that I could dream of marrying."

Mrs. Pegler was still being calm. Hers was a frozen
calm, but frozen calms are better than hysterics. She got
up. It was her intention to go to the big table and there
try to forget. She always found gambling a relief to the
strained nerves.

"Then I can tell you precisely what you are going to do,"

she said. "You are going to pay a fortune in damages to this Trent girl for breach of promise."

If she had yielded to her first impulse and hit him with her bag, she could scarcely have stunned her companion more adequately. Freddie, as Old Nick had mentioned to Jeff, had that odd parsimonious streak in his nature, seen in so many very rich men, which caused him to suffer acute alarm and despondency when his funds were threatened. The fact that he could well afford to pay the most lavish damages for breach of promise to a dozen simultaneous plaintiffs did nothing to alleviate his dismay. His jaw slipped down another notch.

"You think she'll sue me?" he quavered.

"Of course she will sue you."

"A nice girl like that?"

Mrs. Pegler's calm cracked for an instant.

"Don't talk such utter nonsense! Nice girl, indeed! Haven't you the sense to see that she's just an adventuress and that the whole thing was a put-up job between her and that rat?"

This puzzled Freddie. It was the first mention of any rat.

"Which rat?" he asked, seeking more light.

Mrs. Pegler explained that her allusion had been to the Marquis de Maufringneuse et Valerie-Moberanne.

"It's obvious that the two of them planned everything out together. They wanted to get you to that suite so that they could find you there with her and talk you into asking her to marry you, so she told you some absurd story about a burglar."

"There was a burglar. I socked him."

Mrs. Pegler gestured impatiently.

"Well, never mind that," she said. "The point is that owing to that rat's trickery you are going to have to pay this girl goodness knows what. His first move will be to tell

her to bring an action for breach of promise. You won't
have a leg to stand on, and you know what those juries are
like when they get a chance of victimizing a rich man.
You had better start saving your money," said Mrs. Pegler,
and went off to join the Argentines, Portuguese and Greeks
who with tight lips and granite eyes had gathered about the
green board, waiting for the croupier to start the game.

She had been gone some two minutes, when Old Nick
came into the bar.

2

Old Nick, having lunched at the Splendide, for there he
could sign the bill and have it chalked up to Freddie Carpenter, had sauntered across to the Casino and dropped in
at the gambling salon, roaming to and fro and watching the
play with an indulgent eye. There had been a time when
he had been a notable figure in surroundings like these,
flinging his mille notes on the board with the best of them,
but the urge to gamble had left him. What he wanted
now was a cigar, and he had come into the bar to get one.

Observing Freddie, he came over to him and took the
chair at his side.

"Ah, Butch, my boy," he said, puffing affably.

Freddie eyed him askance. Until this moment he had
had this Maufringnooze registered in his mind as a decent
old buck with a nice taste in clothes and a line of conversation to which it was always a pleasure to listen. He saw
him now through Mrs. Pegler's eyes as a rat and a con-
spirer against good young men's bank balances. His
manner, accordingly, when he spoke, was not affectionate.

"Hi!" he said, and as far as it is possible to get scorn,
disgust, loathing and righteous wrath into the mono-
syllable 'Hi!' he got them in.

Old Nick noticed nothing odd in his manner. He blew a carefree smoke-ring.

"I have just been glancing at the *Herald-Tribune*," he said. "They display the news quite prominently, I see. Well, I congratulate you. You are to be envied. You have won a charming girl."

Freddie, unequal to pointing out that he had won two charming girls and was confronted in consequence with a choice between bigamy and a breach of promise suit, glowered in silence.

"And she, too," went on Old Nick, "is to be envied. She has won a fine, open-handed, big-hearted man, a man in a million. Yes, I mean it, Butch. Big-hearted is the word. Not many men would have responded as you did when I approached you. I can never be sufficiently grateful for your generosity."

"What are you talking about?"

"My Umbrella Club which you are financing."

"Your which which I am *what*?"

For the first time, Old Nick found his companion's manner strange. It was as though a tough, unlikeable changeling had been substituted for the genial, amiable Frederick Carpenter with whom it had been so agreeable to have business relations. He was conscious of a nameless fear. He did not like the way things appeared to be shaping.

"We discussed the matter a few days ago," he said, a note of anxiety creeping into his voice, "and you told me you would finance my Umbrella Club."

"Well, I've changed my mind."

Old Nick tottered. It is not easy to totter when sitting down, but he managed it.

"You are not going to finance my Umbrella Club?"

Freddie laughed hackingly. It was one of the most unpleasant sounds Old Nick had ever heard.

"Of course I'm not. A fine chump I should be, financing things with all these heavy expenses I'm having. No, nothing doing," said Freddie, and rose and strode out with vultures gnawing at his bosom. A brisk walk along the Promenade des Anglais might, he thought, do something to restore his composure. At any rate, it would remove him from the orbit of this aristocratic rodent for whom he had conceived so strong a distaste. To hell with all aristocratic rodents, about summed up what he was feeling.

Vultures were gnawing equally briskly at the bosom of the Marquis de Maufringneuse. He was not a man whom it was easy to disconcert, but his normal buoyancy had deserted him completely. His hand, as he raised the cigar mechanically to his lips, quivered like a tuning-fork, and when at this moment a voice spoke from behind him he started so violently that the perfecto nearly flew from his fingers. Turning, he saw Mavis Todd. She was smiling happily, and how anyone could be smiling happily at a time like this was beyond Old Nick.

He sprang up in courtly fashion and knocked his foot against something lying on the floor. Glancing down, he saw that it was a bag, a bag which he recognized as that of his ex-wife, the present Mrs. Winthrop Pegler. What it was doing on the floor of the Casino bar he could not imagine, but he was unable to give the problem thought, for Mavis was speaking.

"Have you seen Freddie?" she said.

A quiver ran through Old Nick. He had indeed seen Freddie.

"He left me a few minutes ago," he replied, and noticed that something was happening to the girl's face. A moment later he realized what it was. She was looking coy. A faint blush mantled her cheek and she drew an arabesque on the carpet with the toe of her shoe.

"Did he tell you?"

"Tell me?"

"We're engaged."

Old Nick goggled at her.

"Engaged?"

"Yes."

"*You* are?   You and Butch?"

"Yes."

A grudging respect for young Mr. Carpenter forced itself on Old Nick.   The boy might have his defects, but he certainly got around.

"Well, well!" he said, overcoming a slight feeling of dizziness.   "This is wonderful news. May I wish you every happiness?"

"Oo, thank you."

"This is a great moment in your life."

"Oo, yes."

"You must be walking on air."

"Oo, I am," said Mavis, and with another of her happy smiles proceeded to do so in the direction of the door.

It was not air that Old Nick walked on as he returned to his seat, it was that bag again.   His foot bumped against it once more, and this time he picked it up and subjected it to a dull-eyed scrutiny.

You cannot subject a bag containing half a million francs to even a dull-eyed scrutiny for long without forming the impression that there is something inside it. Old Nick prodded the bag, and squeezed it, and his conviction deepened that there was cash in this bag.   And if he knew anything of his former wife, of such cash there would be plenty. He was familiar with her practice, when in Casinos, of frequenting the big table in the hope, generally unfulfilled, of skinning the resident dagoes to the bone.

He sat down, meditatively fingering his chin.   A thought had floated into his mind, and it was a thought that called for careful examination from every angle. He opened the bag and scanned its contents, and as he did so became aware of the Tempter at his elbow.

"I would," said the Tempter. "I wouldn't hesitate."

"You wouldn't?" said Old Nick.

"Not for an instant," said the Tempter. "You want capital for your Umbrella Club, and now that Freddie Carpenter has failed you, where else are you going to get it?"

"There is a good deal in what you say."

"And you'll only be borrowing the money. You can pay it back, once the Umbrella Club is a success. And if she has it with her at the big table, she's sure to lose it."

"True."

"So by taking it you will really be doing her a kindness."

"True. True. The only thing is——"

"Can you get away with it? That was what you were about to say, was it not? Of course you can get away with it. Why should anyone suspect you? Woman leaves bag on floor of Casino bar. A hundred people might have taken it. As I see it, you don't enter into the picture at all."

"I think you're right."

"I know I'm right. Here," said the Tempter briskly, "is what I would suggest. Pocket the money and hide the bag behind the cushion of your chair. Then everybody will be happy. Any questions?"

"None," said Old Nick.

A few moments later he was making for the door, his pockets bulging. At the door he met Freddie, coming in.

"Ah, Butch," he said absently.

Freddie gave him a cold look, the sort of look which, if you are not fond of rats, you give one which has said 'Ah, Butch' to you, and hurried on.

3

Setting out on his walk along the Promenade des Anglais, Freddie had suddenly remembered that he had left his mail on the table in the bar at which he had been sitting, and he was hastening now to retrieve it. There was that in his mail which he did not want to have lying about for all eyes to read.

It was still there and, having pocketed the rest of his correspondence, he sat down and with that morbid urge to self-torture which led the priests of Baal to gash themselves with knives started to re-read Terry's note.

It had not changed since he had read it last, nor had the emotions with which he perused it. On first acquaintance it had affected him like the explosion of a hydrogen bomb, and that was how it affected him still.

He sat there in the depths. It is only a man of exceptional strength of character who, having recently become engaged to one girl, can remain wholly unmoved when he discovers that he is also engaged to another. A seasoned wooer like Brigham Young or Henry the Eighth would of course have taken the thing as all in the day's work, scarcely allowing an eyebrow to flicker, but it had left Freddie Carpenter a mere shadow of his former self.

He ran over in his mind a few of the cases of breach of promise which he recalled from his reading of New York's livelier papers and was appalled at the unanimity with which the juries presiding over them had awarded astronomical sums in damages to the various plaintiffs. Archie Bickles, two hundred thousand dollars, if he remembered correctly, and Toddy Van what-was-his-name—the same. Once on the receiving end, a man with anything of a bank balance became a sitting duck for these censors of morals. And Toddy and Archie, compared with him, were practically paupers. A Frederick Carpenter publicized for years as one pre-eminently in the chips would be extremely lucky if he did not find himself trimmed for a matter of half a million.

It was at this point, when he was going down for the third time in his slough of despond, that he was jerked to the surface by a voice at his side and through the same murky mist which had obscured his vision of Mrs. Pegler, perceived a small boy in the uniform of a Ruritanian Field-Marshal.

"Monsieur Carpongtaire?"

The murky mist thinned a little, and Freddie was able to detect that the child was offering him something on a salver. A keener inspection revealed that this was an envelope bearing his name. He took it dully, opened it, glanced at its contents, and instantaneously a number of brass bands of unusual purity and sweetness began playing in every corner of the room. He also fancied that he could hear several choirs of angels in full song, all with silvery voices to which it was a treat to listen.

He beamed at the lad behind the salver. He was aware of a sudden intense affection for the little fellow. He would have liked to ask him his name, his age and his favourite film star and if he hoped to become President some day. Thwarted in this by his ignorance of the French language, he was not cast down. There was something in the way the stripling was holding the salver that suggested to his mind that there were other modes of self-expression. Still beaming, he placed a mille note on it, and Ruritania's favourite Field-Marshal, thanking him profusely and unintelligibly, withdrew to rejoin his army. And Freddie, having re-read the contents of the envelope, just to make sure that his first perusal had been correct, raised his eyes thankfully to heaven.

On the way to heaven they fell on a figure standing

at the bar, in conversation with the man behind it, and recognizing Terry, at the extreme limit of his lungs he uttered the word 'Hoy!'

It was of sandwiches and a glass of milk that Terry was speaking to the man behind the bar. Having bought her plane tickets and drawn the remainder of her money from the bank, she had become conscious of a gnawing sensation, due partly to the vultures which were being so busy today and partly to the fact that packing and ticket-buying had caused her to go without lunch. Her heart was broken, but she was a healthy girl, and round about the hour of two-thirty healthy girls who have missed their lunch feel, no matter how broken-hearted they are, the need for a sand-wich. She and the barman had got the sandwich end of the thing straight, but she was having a little difficulty in con-vincing him that when she spoke of drinking milk, she was serious.

Freddie's 'Hoy', coming out of the void, startled both of them. Terry, first to recover, spun round, stared, gathered from his gestures that he would have speech with her, and reluctantly, for she had no desire to talk to Freddie or anyone, walked over to the table and took the chair whose cushion had so recently been honoured by the pressure of Old Nick's beautifully cut trouser-seat. The barman, glad to be done with all this loose talk of milk as a beverage, gave a relieved sigh and started polishing glasses.

"Hello," said Freddie buoyantly. "Nice afternoon."

"If you like this sort of afternoon," said Terry.

"I've just been reading your note."

"Which note? The second one?"

"Yup. The one saying you aren't going to marry me."

Terry felt an apology would be in order.

"I'm sorry," she said.

"I'm not," said Freddie, even more buoyantly than before, "because on the strength of having been given the

brusheroo by you that night I went and got en aged to
Mavis Todd."

"Really?"

"You betcher. Underneath a pine tree in the undergrowth at the fifteenth hole."

"Why, Freddie, I'm delighted."

"Me, too. You're sure," said Freddie in sudden
alarm, "there isn't another on the way?"

"Another what?"

"Another of these inter-office memos saying you've
changed your mind again and do want to marry me?"

Terry's gloom lightened a little. A conversation with
Freddie always cheered her up.

"No, that's the last one. The five-star final."

"Well, that's swell," said Freddie, relieved. "You can
understand it's quite a strain for a fellow, finding he's
engaged to two girls at the same time."

"It must be. I suppose everything went black?"

"Blackish. Yup. Still, no need to talk about it now.
There's one thing, though, that puzzled me a good deal. I
couldn't make out what you wanted to marry me *for*."

"Why, Freddie, you're fascinating."

"I dare say, but it still doesn't make sense. You told
me you were that way about Jeff."

Terry felt, as Mrs. Pegler had done, a momentary urge
to hit her companion over the head with her bag. Like
Mrs. Pegler, she overcame it.

"When you are a little older, Freddie dear," she said
patiently, "you will know that it sometimes happens that a
girl is that way about a man, but the man isn't that way
about her. I mean nothing in Jeff's life. You see, I
haven't any money."

"Eh?"

"Not to speak of. My father wrote plays, and one of
them has been dug up and they are doing it on television,

and I got two thousand dollars out of the deal, so I decided to spend it having a brief good time in this Mecca of the fashionable world."

"This what?"

"That's what the guide-books call Roville, the Jewel of Picardy and the Mecca of the fashionable world. Though where they pick up these expressions, I couldn't tell you. I suppose they see them scrawled on walls and fences."

Freddie was adjusting his mind to this unexpected revelation.

"I always thought you were rolling in the stuff."

"So did Jeff. When he found I wasn't, he was off over the horizon like a jack rabbit. You couldn't see him for dust."

"You mean he's gone?"

"We had a date for dinner last night, and I got a polite note from him, breaking it. He said he had been called away on business and couldn't say when he would be coming back. Meaning, of course, that he wouldn't be coming back."

Freddie's was a mind that liked to take its time over things, and it was not immediately that he perceived the flaw in her reasoning. He knew the flaw was there, but it eluded him. Then he got it.

"But he must be coming back. He borrowed my car."

"Borrowed your car?"

"Sure. He called me up that night and said he had a lunch next day in Paris with some publisher and could he have my car. I said Yup, of course he could, and he went off in it. I'll tell you what I'll do," said Freddie. "I'll run over to the hotel and see if the car's there."

He hurried off, all zeal and anxiety to help, and something stirred in Terry's heart. It was a small, faint hope, at the moment scarcely to be called a hope at all, but giving indications that if encouraged it would grow. She refused to encourage it, just as on that long ago afternoon at Bensonburg she had refused to encourage the hope that the prominent network would purchase the television rights of *Brother Masons*. The more you hoped, the more you were disappointed. To take her mind off the thing, she went to the bar and once more put in her order for sandwiches, to be accompanied this time, she told the barman, by brandy and soda. She was feeling weak and in need of a stimulant. The barman, reaching for the brandy bottle, gave the impression that a weight had rolled off his mind. He put the refreshment on a tray, and Terry, returning to the table, sat back in her chair, beginning to feel restored.

If you sit back in a chair behind the cushion of which a French Marquis had thrust a bag belonging to his former wife, it is inevitable that sooner or later you will feel that you are not as comfortable as you could wish. You become aware that some solid substance is intruding on your spine, and you rise and investigate.

Terry did this and, groping behind the cushion, found her fingers closing on something which she was unable to identify till, pulling it out, she saw that it was a bag, an ornate, expensive bag whose aspect was somehow oddly familiar. She was sure she had seen it before, but where she could not say. It was Chester Todd, coming at this moment to the table with drawn face and lack-lustre eyes, who supplied the information.

"Oh, excuse me," said Chester diffidently, for though he was convinced that he had met this girl somewhere, they had not been introduced and he was a great stickler for etiquette and the proprieties. "You don't happen by any chance to have seen a . . . Oh, you've got it. That's fine. Mrs. Pegler's bag," he explained. "She thought she must have left it in here. She sent me to find it."

"Of course," said Terry. "It's hers, isn't it? I knew I had seen it."

"Thanks," said Chester, taking it. He hesitated for a moment, then, feeling that it would hardly be correct to inaugurate a quiz, turned to go. "Sorry I had to bother you," he said.

"Not at all," said Terry.

Freddie came galloping back. His face showed that he was bearing good tidings.

"Oh, hello, Chester," he said. "Say, it's all right," he went on, turning to Terry. "The car's there."

Terry's heart leaped.

"Oh, Freddie!"

Freddie turned back to Chester.

"You don't understand all this," he said. "It's just that we thought someone had gone away, and he hasn't."

"No," said Terry happily, "we must have been thinking of a couple of other fellows."

4

There was a dazed look on Chester Todd's pale face as he made his way back to the gambling salon. He had had a shock, and, like Othello, was perplexed in the extreme. He found Mrs. Pegler at the *caisse*, cashing a cheque, her third that afternoon. She had the morose air of one who has found the process of trying to skin the dagoes to the bone unprofitable. Her losses, taken in conjunction with her niece's future husband's prospective breach of promise suit, had left her soured.

"Say, listen," said Chester.

"Have you got my bag?" said Mrs. Pegler.

"Yes, I've got it, but listen. You know that girl, the one that's engaged to Freddie."

"Frederick is engaged to Mavis."

"No, no, you keep making that mistake," said Chester

patiently. "He's engaged to this girl named Trent. Only her name isn't Trent."

"Oh, don't drivel, Chester."

"I'm not drivelling. Her name's Fellowes, and she's the maid of the Miss Trent I met at St. Rocque."

Mrs. Pegler stared.

"What on earth do you mean?"

"I told you I knew I had seen her before somewhere. It was at Miss Trent's suite. She was serving the cocktails."

Mrs. Pegler drew a deep breath.

"Are you sure of this?"

"Quite sure. I found her with your bag and we got talking, and then Freddie came along and said something about somebody who they thought had gone away not having gone away after all, and this girl laughed merrily and said they must have been thinking of a couple of other fellows. And then it all came back to me. I remembered that afternoon at Miss Trent's suite. I remembered saying 'That's an extraordinary pretty maid you've got', and Miss Trent said 'Fellowes? Oh, yes, quite attractive', or words to that effect. Odd how one's memory works. Don't you think so?"

Mrs. Pegler forbore to discuss the eccentricities of memory. Her air of gloom had vanished.

"Why, this alters everything!"

"Eh?"

"It's too long to explain, but Frederick has got himself involved with this girl and has put himself in a position where she can sue him for breach of promise. . . ."

Chester blinked.

"*Freddie* has?"

"Yes. Apparently he asked her to marry him, and then got engaged to Mavis."

Chester blinked again.

"He's engaged to both of them, you mean?"

"Yes."

"I hadn't a notion he was such a dasher," said Chester, marvelling. "I often say that half the world doesn't know how the other two-thirds live."

Mrs. Pegler continued to simmer joyfully.

"It was a dreadful situation, but, as I say, what you tell me alters everything. What jury is going to give her damages when they find that she is a maid, who has been masquerading as her mistress? You are absolutely certain that this is the girl you saw at St. Rocque?"

"Oh, quite. But what beats me is how, if she's just a maid, she can afford a suite at the Splendide."

"No doubt she has her resources," said Mrs. Pegler grimly. Then her former sunniness returned. "Well, this is wonderful," she said. "I have a feeling that this is going to change my luck."

"Been losing?"

"All the time. But it will be better now. Give me my bag."

"Here you are."

Mrs. Pegler was smiling as she held out her hand, but the smile faded like breath off a mirror.

"What does this mean?" she said sharply.

"Eh?" said Chester, wincing.

"This bag is empty!"

"Shouldn't it be?"

"Of course it shouldn't. It had five hundred thousand francs in it. Where did you find it?"

"I didn't find it. The Trent-Fellowes combination had it. She was at the table, and I came up and said: 'Oh, excuse me, you don't happen by any chance to have seen a . . .' and then I saw she was grasping the bag. So I took it off her and went along."

Mrs. Pegler was struggling with feelings for a moment too deep for words. Then she found speech.

"Well!"

"Eh?"

Mrs. Pegler laughed bitterly.

"I said she had resources, but I did not think they came from stealing money. Chester, get me a taxi!"

"Where are you going?"

"To the police!" said Mrs. Pegler.

CHAPTER TEN

CROSSING the Casino terrace on her way back to the hotel, Terry came to a sudden halt. She had seen before her, standing with his head bowed as if in thought, a man of maximum stoutness who looked exactly like the Mr. Clutterbuck at whose summer home in Bensonburg she had so often delivered baskets of eggs and combs of honey. Then he raised his head, and she saw that the reason he looked so like Mr. Clutterbuck was that he was Mr. Clutterbuck.

"Why, hello!" she said, amazed. It is disconcerting for a girl to find Clutterbucks where no Clutterbucks should be.

He gave her an owl-like stare, his chins swaying in the breeze.

"Wait!" he said, holding up a hand as if he were directing traffic. "Don't tell me. Begins with a J., and you run that farm in Tuttle's Lane and charge a damn sight too much for honey. Jones? Jackson? Jenkins?"

"Try Trent."

"Trent!" said Russell Clutterbuck, flashing his spectacles triumphantly. "I knew I'd get it. Trent's the name, and you're the one they call Terry."

"Short for Teresa."

"Short, as you say, for Teresa. What on earth are you doing here?"

"Just taking a little holiday. The Trent family came into some money the other day and we thought we would travel and broaden our minds. Kindly neighbours are looking after the farm.   But I never expected to see you so far from Bensonburg."

"I had business in Paris."

"This isn't Paris.   It's Roville-sur-Mer."

"Well, there's no law saying a man can't come to Roville-sur-Mer, if he wants to, is there?" said Russell Clutterbuck belligerently.   Then, as if feeling he had been too harsh, "Sorry if I seem grouchy.   I've a lot on my mind, and I didn't get any sleep last night, and I came all the way from Paris in a hired car driven by a lunatic whose dearest wish appeared to be to commit suicide.   We only touched the ground about twice.   If you really want to know why I'm here, I'm looking for a young fellow called the Comte d'Escrignon."

"What!"

"Okay, okay, maybe I *didn't* pronounce it right.   Who cares?"

"Do you know Jeff?"

"Never heard of him."

"I mean the Comte d'Escrignon."

"There you are, you said it just the way I did.   Call him Jeff, do you?   Certainly I know him.   We lunched together in Paris yesterday, and I saw him off in his car at seven this morning after a bowl of onion soup.   Roville-sur-Mer he said he was headed for, but the poor fish forgot to mention where he was staying, so now I've got to hunt through every hotel in the darned place, I suppose."

"You won't have to do that.   He's at the Splendide, about a hundred yards from here."

"I can manage a hundred yards," said Russell Clutterbuck, the old athlete.   "Well, it's a bit of luck, him being a friend of yours.   Known him long?"

"Only since I came to Roville."

"Fine young fellow.   Fought in the Macky and all that. Clever, too."

"Yes, he's written a book."

"I know he's written a book. I'm publishing it."

"Oh, Mr. Clutterbuck!"

"What do you mean, 'Oh, Mr. Clutterbuck'?"

Terry said she had meant Oh, Mr. Clutterbuck.

"It's such wonderful news," she explained. "It will start him off with a bang. You're such a splendid publisher."

"None better," agreed Mr. Clutterbuck, cordially.

"May I kiss you?"

"No, you may not. Holy smoke, do you think I've time to stand around getting kissed by girls? I've got to see this boy immediately on a matter of the utmost importance. Every moment is precious."

"You wouldn't care to come to my suite and have a drink first?"

Russell Clutterbuck licked his lips. Her words had conjured up a pleasant picture. Then a wary look crept into the eyes behind the spectacles.

"Is your sister there?"

"Which sister? Jo went home. Kate's there."

"I mean the one who looks at you like a Duchess looking at a potato bug."

"That's Kate."

"Then I think I'll skip it. Last time I saw her, we had a little tiff about the price of honey, and I wouldn't want to meet her again, if not absolutely necessary."

"Suppose I phone you if the coast is clear?"

"Do. You'll find me in that young fellow's room. What's his number?"

"The desk clerk will tell you."

"I keep forgetting that they have desk clerks in France. You wouldn't expect them to be so civilized. All right, give me a ring."

"There's just one thing, though. If he didn't leave you

till seven in the morning and then had that long drive, he's
probably asleep."

"I'll wake him. I'll wake him with a wet sponge. I've
woken better men than him with wet sponges," said
Russell Clutterbuck with quiet confidence.

Terry was smiling happily as she went into her suite,
for she had enjoyed this exchange of ideas with one of
Bensonburg's brightest minds, but she ceased to smile when
she saw Kate or, to be accurate, heard her. Kate, in-
visible in her bedroom, was plainly engaged in packing her
effects against the journey home, and for the first time the
thought occurred to Terry that this elder sister of hers,
apprised of the fact that there was not going to be any
journey home, might display the less amiable side of her
nature. Kate rather readily took umbrage, and when she
did had no diffidence about showing it.

She coughed an embarrassed cough, and Kate's voice
came from the bedroom.

"Is that you, Terry?"

"Yes, ma'am."

"Did you get the tickets?"

"Er—yes. Yes, I got the tickets."

"Good. I'm nearly through with my packing. When
do we start?"

"We don't start," said Terry in a small voice. "We're
not going."

There was dead silence in the bedroom, a silence that
made it plain that there was an overwrought soul on the
premises. It seemed to Terry's guilty mind to last for
several minutes. Then Kate emerged.

"What did you say?" she said, looking like the head-
mistress of a girls' school, who has come upon one of her
young charges smoking in the shrubbery. "We're not
going?"

"No."

"You mean that you have changed your mind *again*?"

"Yes.   You see——"

Kate turned and went back into the bedroom.   When she came out, she was wearing a hat.   She gave Terry one long awful look and strode from the room in silence.   No words were needed to explain that she was about to take another of her walks on the Promenade des Anglais in the hope—the faint hope—of restoring herself to composure. The door slammed, and Terry went to the telephone to inform Mr. Clutterbuck that his path had been made straight.   She then used the instrument to order from Room Service two bottles of the best champagne.   If Russell Clutterbuck was going to publish Jeff's book, nothing meaner than champagne was good enough for him, and from what she had heard of Mr. Clutterbuck she thought that two bottles would be about the right amount.

She found herself giggling feebly.   She was a clear-thinking girl and had no difficulty in realizing what a trial she must be to poor Kate.   So it had been from childhood's earliest hour and so it would be, she feared, when they were both old and grey.   Her small consolation was the reflection that Jo had always maddened the head of the family even more than she did.

2

Jeff was not asleep when Russell Clutterbuck found him, and the latter had no need to put into effect his kindly plan of waking him with a wet sponge.   He had bathed and dressed and was enjoying a belated breakfast.   The sight of his visitor gave him a momentary feeling that he had fallen asleep again and was dreaming.

"Mr. Clutterbuck!" he exclaimed.

"Call me Russ," said the publisher. He, too, seemed astonished. The look which he was directing at the table was the look of one who can scarcely believe his eyes. "Coffee and rolls!" he said. "Is that all you have for lunch?"

"This is breakfast."

"Well, for breakfast."

"That's all."

"Good God!" said Russell Clutterbuck, and muttered something under his breath about sending it to Ripley. He mopped his brow. "Well," he said, "you're probably surprised to see me."

"I am a little. Though delighted, of course. What brings you here?"

"I came because I'm in a spot, Jeff, and you've got to help me out of it. I need service and co-operation worse than any man has ever needed service and co-operation in the history of the human race." He took the remains of a roll from the tray, added butter and subsided into a chair like some prehistoric monster settling down in its swamp. "It's Mrs. Clutterbuck," he said. "Bad news, very bad news, the worst possible news. A great shock it's been to me. I'm trembling like a leaf."

Partly from emotion and partly because the roll impeded clearness of diction, he spoke so sepulchrally that Jeff started, wondering what this could portend. He was aware that his companion's life partner was suffering from mumps, and he had never heard of mumps taking a fatal turn, but there was always, of course, the possibility.

"She's not . . .?" He paused, seeking words. "Mrs. Clutterbuck is—er—still with us?"

"You bet she's still with us. With her hair in a braid."

The telephone rang. Mr. Clutterbuck, being within reach of it, took up the receiver.

"Hello? Oh, it's you. Gone, has she? Fine. I'll

be with you as soon as I can make it. Right now I'm in conference. Girl I know back home wants me to come and have a drink," he said, hanging up. "Yes, Mrs. Clutterbuck is still with us, all right, and, if you ask me, biting slices out of the furniture. Say, do you know what causes half the trouble in this world? That thing of the time being different in America and Europe."

"Five hours earlier in America, you mean?"

"Exactly. When it's three in the morning in Paris, it's ten the night before on Long Island. So what happens? Mrs. Clutterbuck, over there in Bensonburg, forgetting that and finding herself at a loose end around about ten, puts in a call to say Hello to me. Doesn't get me, of course. Tries again at eleven. No answer. Then she suddenly remembers about the difference in the time, and when I got back to the Ritz after leaving you, I found she'd been calling up steadily till two in the morning."

"Seven o'clock in Paris."

"Seven o'clock in Paris," echoed Clutterbuck hollowly. "Did you tell me you were married?"

"Not yet. Hoping to be."

"Hoping?" Russell Clutterbuck gave him a puzzled look, and finished his piece of roll. "Well, when you're a married man, you'll know that if a wife calls her husband up in Paris till seven in the morning and he isn't there, that husband is going to have to do some quick explaining."

"I can imagine."

"If Mrs. Clutterbuck finds out that I was in the town all night, she'll leap to the conclusion that I was out getting plastered and I shall never hear the end of it. You know and I know that I was as sober as a judge, but . . . What are you looking like that for?"

"Was I looking like that? I'm sorry. I was just thinking of that last place we went into before we had the onion soup. The one where there was an American barman."

"I recall the place you mean. What about it?"

"You wouldn't say you were a little animated there?"

"Not in the least. What gave you that impression?"

"Well, you kissed the barman, if you remember, and then you and he sang 'Old Man River' in close harmony."

Russell Clutterbuck drew himself up with a good deal of dignity.

"Perfectly understandable behaviour. We had got talking, and in the course of our conversation he chanced to mention that he had been born in Niles, Michigan, my home town. Naturally, one marked the occasion with a certain amount of quiet rejoicing. It isn't every day that you meet a barman from your home town, especially when you're miles away from civilization. But forget about him and concentrate on the vital problem. When Mrs. Clutterbuck asks where I was all night, what do I tell her?"

"Ah!"

"I should have thought you could have done better than 'Ah!' said Russell Clutterbuck reproachfully. "A clever young fellow like you. What's the good of being an author if you can't make up a story? Come on, my boy, let's have some service."

Thus stimulated, Jeff found his brain cells functioning briskly. After twice starting to speak and then stopping and saying 'No, that wouldn't do', he was able to announce that he thought he had got it.

"What did you do after lunch yesterday?" he said.

Russell Clutterbuck made the sort of gesture a man makes when in conference with one of the Jukes family.

"You know what I did. You were there. I went to sleep."

Jeff shook his head.

"No. That is where you are mistaken. Directly after lunch you got into my car and I drove you to Roville. If

you remember, one or two rather tricky points had come
up in connection with this book of mine, and I was unable
to stay on in Paris and discuss them, because my father was
sick down here and I was nursing him, so you thought the
only way out of the difficulty was for you to come to
Roville. How's that?"

"Genius."

"Plausible, I think?"

"Very plausible."

"If a man has a sick father in Roville, you can't keep him
hanging about in Paris."

"Not human. Un-American. Have you a sick father?"

"I have a father, though not sick."

"He's a Comte, too, I suppose?"

"No, a Marquis. That's a little higher in the social
scale. The Marquis de Maufringneuse et Valerie-
Moberanne."

"Gosh! Mrs. Clutterbuck will eat that!"

"So now you see why she couldn't get you on the phone.
All the time she was trying to reach you at the Ritz in Paris,
you were tucked up in bed at the Splendide in Roville.
One of those amusing little misunderstandings. She'll
laugh her head off. Of course, that's just the rough story
outline. There may be a certain amount of polishing work
to be done."

"I'll leave you to it. I'll go and contact this girl who
wants me to have a drink, and you be studying that story
from every angle. Test each link in it. Examine it for
holes. If there's anything in it that doesn't add up right, I
want to know before we pass the galley proofs. See you later,
Jeff."

"I'll be counting the minutes, Russ."

Left alone, Jeff should have directed the full force of his
intellect to the Clutterbuck story, its possible holes and the
strength of its claims to add up right, testing, as the other

had put it, every link. But he found his thoughts straying off to Terry.

Women till now had played a rather minor part in Jeff's life. They had always attracted him, but they had not been important. They came and went. You loved them, if loved was the word, and after a while they let you down or you just parted amicably. One way or the other, it had never mattered much. It had all been a sort of game.

But at heart he was a romantic, and he had always known that somewhere, waiting, was the one girl, the golden girl, the other half of himself that every romantic prays for, and in Terry, from the first meeting on the yacht, he was convinced that he had found her. 'I wandered through a world of women, seeking you,' said the poet, and Jeff felt how true that was. And there was another poet who said 'Once you're kissed by Amy, tear up the list, it's Amy,' and that was true, too. These poets hit the nail on the head.

The ringing of the telephone broke in on his meditations. It was Archie Brice, his friend on the *Herald-Tribune*. His voice was reproachful.

"Where on earth have you been?" he asked. "I was trying to get you all yesterday."

Jeff said he had been in Paris, seeing the sights with his publisher.

"My *P*ublisher, Archie," he said, dignifying the word with a capital letter. "Clutterbuck, God bless him, the man you very kindly wrote to on my behalf. He's taken the book."

"Well, that's fine. How was the old boy?"

"Very festive."

"Appetite good?"

"Excellent."

"He'll burst some day. But I didn't call up to talk about him. In your wanderings around Roville have you happened to run into Freddie Carpenter, the Fizzo man?"

"I'm his guest."

"You are?   Then you must know the girl."

"What girl?"

"The girl he's engaged to."

"Engaged? I knew nothing of this. When did it happen?"

"The night before last.   Somebody tipped us off after we'd gone to press.   It's in today's paper.   Well, anyone as rich as Freddie is news, so what we want is an interview with the girl, full of human interest—who she is, where they met and all that sort of thing.   Go after the wench and make her talk."

Jeff laughed.

"Nobody can make Mavis Todd talk.   She never says anything except 'Yes, Auntie'."

"Who's Mavis Todd?"

"Isn't she the girl he's engaged to?"

"No, her name's not Todd.   I'm pretty sure of that. It's somebody called . . .   Wait a second, I'm looking for the paper . . . it's somebody called Trent.   T-r-e-n-t," said Archie Brice.   "First name, Teresa."

3

After telephoning Room Service for the champagne, Terry sat for a while musing on Kate and wondering, for she was tender-hearted, what she could do to atone.

Chocolates?

No, Kate despised chocolates.

Flowers?

No, Kate thought flowers a foolish extravagance.

It was a difficult problem, and she was still trying to solve it when the bell rang.   Answering it in the expectation of seeing Russell Clutterbuck, she found Old Nick on the mat.

Old Nick's first move on leaving the Casino had been to go to the best garage in the town and hire a car. He had been greatly impressed by the Grenouillière at Aumale on the previous night and it would be pleasant, he thought, now that he was in funds, to dine there again after a leisurely trip about the countryside. He had been on the point of starting, when there had flashed into his mind a thought.

It was the same thought which had come to Mrs. Pegler and which she had handed on to Freddie Carpenter—the thought that if ever any girl had been in a position to bring the perfect breach of promise suit, that girl was Terry, and it was not only a duty but a pleasure to him to go and point this out to her.

He was filled with a quiet elation. It seemed to him that everything was for the best in this best of all possible worlds. His son Jefferson loved this girl. The girl loved his son Jefferson. The sole obstacle in the way of married bliss was their mutual lack of money, and this obstacle Frederick Carpenter would now remove. With half a million dollars or so transferred from the bank account of Frederick Carpenter to that of the bride-to-be, all would be wedding bells and orange blossom and happiness.

As he entered the suite, he had seldom felt cheerier, but one has to comport oneself fittingly on these occasions, so it was with a mournful gravity that he took her hand and patted it.

"My dear child," he said in a hushed voice. His manner would not have been out of place if they had been meeting at the funeral of a mutual friend. "I'm afraid I bring bad news, my dear. Prepare yourself for a shock. Frederick Carpenter proposed marriage to you, did he not?"

"Yes. He said you advised it."

"I did. I assured him it was the only course open to a man of honour. Unfortunately it turns out that Frederick

Carpenter is not a man of honour, but a heartless scoundrel. I have just learned that he has become engaged to my former wife's niece, Mavis Todd."

"Yes, he told me."

Old Nick started.

"He told you? On the telephone, of course?" he said, thinking what he would have done in Freddie's place.

"No, in the Casino bar."

"Face to face? Are there no limits to this man's effrontery?" said Old Nick, plainly wondering what the younger generation was coming to. "But you must not despair," he went on patting her hand again. "There is a bright side. You will now instantly bring a suit against him for breach of promise."

"*Me?*"

"Of course. My dear child, you have what my son Jefferson would call an open and shut case. Owing to my foresight in telephoning the news of your engagement to the *Paris Herald-Tribune*——"

"You didn't!"

"It was my first move. The announcement is in the paper today. This will carry extraordinary weight with the jury. I shall be much surprised if you are not awarded several hundred thousand dollars in damages. And a very good thing, too," said Old Nick virtuously. "These dissolute young millionaires need a sharp lesson. They must be taught that they cannot go about breaking innocent girls' hearts with impunity."

"But my heart isn't broken. I'm feeling fine."

"Please, please!" said Old Nick urgently. "Do please be careful not to let anyone hear you talking like that. It would be fatal. You are distraught. You are inconsolable. You contemplate suicide. Can you weep?"

"I don't often."

"Practise it. Nothing makes a surer impression.

Twice—no, thrice—I have been present in court while my friend Prince Blamont-Chevry was being sued for breach of promise, and each time the plaintiff melted the jury with her tears, causing them to award double the amount of damages which might have been expected. And none of those plaintiffs had as good a case as yours."

"Would you say my case was good?"

"Open and shut."

"I wonder. I think I may have weakened it."

"What do you mean? How?"

"By writing Freddie a letter saying I wouldn't marry him."

Old Nick reeled.

"You did that? You wrote him a *letter*?"

"Yes. He seemed very pleased about it. I got the impression that it had relieved his mind."

With tottering steps Old Nick made for the table on which the champagne stood. He poured out a glass and drained it.

His hopes and dreams were in ruins about him. In a career liberally studded with the bludgeonings of chance he could recall none more shattering than this.

It was consequently to an atmosphere of gloom and strain that Russell Clutterbuck entered a few moments later. But he was much too happy to notice it. The one thing a publisher likes is a good story, and the more he ran Jeff's contribution over in his mind, the better it seemed to him. Mrs. Clutterbuck was a severe critic and on several occasions had refused to set the seal of her approval on some of his own efforts, but he could not see her tearing this one apart. In Russell Clutterbuck's opinion it had everything, and he was at the peak of his effervescence. Few sunnier publishers can ever have crossed the threshold of a seashore hotel suite. He greeted Terry with a cheerful whoop and, introduced to Old Nick, complimented him warmly on having such a son, as fine a young fellow as he had ever met and one who—a rarity in Russell Clutterbuck's experience —though handicapped by being a Frenchman, did not louse things up by talking French all the time.

"That boy has brains," he said. "He will go far. Hello, are those caramels in that box there?" He walked over to the table and extracted one with a skilful finger and thumb. A man should always take in a certain amount of energy-giving food at regular intervals. "Oh, say, Terry Trent, can I use your phone? I want to put in a trans-atlantic call to Mrs. Clutterbuck."

It was while he was urging Exchange to get him Benson-burg 0231 and Terry was trying to persuade him that he would obtain better results by saying Bon-son-boorg zero deux trois un, that the door bell rang and Terry's heart gave a leap. Was this Jeff?

It was not. It was a very large man with a very red neck and beetling eyebrows. One of the eyes beneath these eyebrows was an angry purple.

"Mademoiselle Tur-rente?"

"Yes."

"A word with you, mademoiselle," said Commissaire Boissonade, and strode weightily into the room, looking like a sheriff in a Western B picture.

4

When Mrs. Pegler, accompanied by a reluctant Chester Todd, burst into his office as he sat digesting his lunch, she had found Pierre Alexandre Boissonade in sombre mood, his brows bent, his fingers twitching, his manner that of one who is allergic to Peglers. Unjustly perhaps, he considered her responsible for the *marron* at which he had twice that morning caught M. Punez looking with what had seemed to him something gloating in his gaze, and not even the thought of the five hundred dollars which he had prudently secured in advance was enough to soften his conviction that she was a pest and a menace. He had a prejudice against Americans, and she did nothing to remove it.

But as she told her sensational story, animation came into his face and the eye which was still open gleamed with a strange light. Her words were music to his ears. This, he felt, was the stuff. No more nebulous suspicions of the Tur-rente woman but a case against her which, as Old Nick would have said, was open and shut. Here at last he told himself, was something solid, something a commissaire of police could get his teeth into.

It was with an offensive air of self-satisfaction, therefore, that he now took up his stand in the centre of the room, one hand resting on the table, the other hanging at his side all ready to point an intimidating finger at the Tur-rente woman as she cowered before his remorseless questioning. This was his hour.

At the moment, she was not cowering. His official bearing and that purple eye had told her who this must be, and she looked at him with a proud distaste.

"Mademoiselle, I am Boissonade, Commissaire of Police."

"I thought you were. And you want a word with me, you said. Well?"

"Might I see Mademoiselle's passport?"

"It's in my bag."

"And the bag?"

"On the table there beside you."

"Thank you, mademoiselle."

He opened the bag, spilling its contents on the table. Taking up the passport, he studied it grimly.

"It's in order, isn't it?"

M. Boissonade unloosed his first thunderbolt.

"No, mademoiselle, it is very far from being in order. This passport is made out to Therese Tur-rente. And your name," said M. Boissonade, dropping the mademoiselle, for the time for civilities was past, "is Fellowes." He shot a look at her. "You are amused, one perceives," he said unpleasantly. "You smile!"

"I'm sorry. Go on."

"Fellowes," repeated M. Boissonade, returning to the matter in hand. "And testimony has been given that establishes that while at St. Rocque on the Breton coast you were the maid of Mademoiselle Tur-rente. Am I right?"

"In a way."

"I do not understand this 'in a way'. Were you or were you not? Yes or no?"

"Yes."

"Good. It would have been useless for you to deny it. You have been identified by witnesses. So we proceed. In St. Rocque you are Fellowes, the maid. Here—in Roville—you are Mademoiselle Tur-rente. This gives one to think. We ask ourselves, do we not—what has become of the real Mademoiselle Tur-rente?"

"She went back to America."

"Leaving you with her name, her clothes, and her money? Of course, of course. What could be more natural?"

"Do you think I murdered her?"

It was precisely what M. Boissonade did think and had been thinking ever since Chester Todd had given his headache-racked evidence. Disappearances of lonely American women, quietly put away for their money and jewels by miscreants engaged by them as maids or chauffeurs or whatever it might be, were a commonplace in the annals of French crime. There were two or three of them every year, and they always got a good display in the papers. M. Boissonade looked forward brightly to seeing himself in print with photograph inset.

"That," he said ponderously, "we shall ascertain."

Russell Clutterbuck had been regarding M. Boissonade during these exchanges with growing disfavour. The Commissaire's intrusion had spoiled what was promising to be a pleasant party, all friends together and everybody cutting up and having a nice time.

"Who is this son of a bachelor?" he asked, giving him the cold stare he would have given a best-selling author who had transferred his allegiance from the firm of Winch and Clutterbuck to some rival publishing house. "Looks to me like a sharecropper."

He had addressed the question to Old Nick, but Old Nick was still in a sort of stupor. It was Terry who replied.

"He's the Commissaire of Police."

"Great Scott!" said Russell Clutterbuck, intrigued. "Has the joint been pinched?"

Old Nick recovered himself sufficiently to try to explain.

"He is saying that Miss Trent's name is Fellowes."

Mr. Clutterbuck detected the flaw in this immediately. He was a quick thinker.

"How can her name be Fellowes when it's Trent?"

"He says it is not Trent."

"Of course it's Trent."

"You can vouch for this?"

"Till the cows come home. I know her well. She's been supplying me with honey for years at, in my opinion, far too high a price. A lot of nonsense about the wear and tear on the bees."

"The Commissaire insists that she is Miss Trent's maid."

"Her *what*? The man must be blotto."

M. Boissonade rapped on the table. He strongly objected to the presence of a studio audience at what should have been a private audition, and it offended him that these superfluous persons should be talking English. It was a language he despised and disapproved of, considering it to bear too close a resemblance to the meaningless twittering of birds.

"*Parlez français, monsieur!*" he thundered.

Mr. Clutterbuck gave him another of his cold looks.

"What's the sense of saying 'Parley frongsay'? How the hell can I parley frongsay? Hey, Terry Trent."

"Yes, Mr. Clutterbuck?"

"Tell that fool with the bunged-up eye he's crazy. Though who isn't in this darned country? I never met a Frenchman yet who had all his marbles."

M. Boissonade continued to regard the intruders with a hostile eye.

"Who are these persons?"

"Friends of mine," said Terry. "The short, stout one is Mr. Clutterbuck, an American publisher, the tall thin one is the Marquis de Maufringneuse."

M. Boissonade softened for an instant. He was a fervent admirer of the aristocracy. Then he congealed again. Business was business.

"I await your explanation," he said.

"Here it comes," said Terry. "You don't speak English, Monsieur Boissonade?"

"I do not."

"Then you won't have understood what Mr. Clutterbuck was saying, especially as his mouth was full. Mr. Clutterbuck has his summer home in the village in America where I live. He has known me for years, and he says my name is Trent. You can take it, therefore, that it is Trent. Teresa Trent, but think of me as Terry, Monsieur Boissonade, because I feel that we are going to be great, great friends. I see you've hurt your eye. I can't tell you how sorry I am. Did you run into something in the dark?"

M. Boissonade refused to be diverted to a discussion of his eye. It was a subject on which he was reticent.

"Witnesses have testified that your name is Fellowes. You yourself have admitted it."

"I'm coming to the Fellowes part. It's rather a complicated story, and you will have to attend very closely. Try to imagine, monsieur, that you are two girls living on a chicken farm."

M. Boissonade blinked. He found the assignment a difficult one.

"Yearning," proceeded Terry, "for a glimpse of the great world outside. One day, out of a blue sky, you get a little unexpected money. What do you do? You say to yourself that now is your chance to buy some Paris clothes and have a holiday in France. Ah, la belle France!" said Terry, kissing her hand.

"I got that," said Mr. Clutterbuck in a confidential aside to Old Nick. "She said 'Ah, la belle Fronks'. That means 'Beautiful France', he explained kindly.

"But there was a difficulty. We couldn't afford a set of Paris clothes each, we had to make one set do for both of us. So we arranged it that one of us should have a month all dressed up as the rich Miss Trent, while the other acted as her maid. Then at the end of the month, we would change places and go somewhere else. We cut cards for first choice, and my sister won and chose St. Rocque for her month. That is why I was Fellowes in St. Rocque and am Miss Trent here. I hope I haven't made your head swim?"

"Not at all, mademoiselle."

"You understand now?"

"Perfectly." M. Boissonade seemed positively amiable.

He achieved something approaching a smile. "An ingenious idea."

"We thought so."

"You had not much money, you say?"

"Not a great deal."

"And you found living at these fashionable resorts expensive?"

"Very."

"I can well believe it. And so," said M. Boissonade, turning off his amiability, as if he had pressed a switch, "when the opportunity presented itself of stealing five hundred thousand francs from the bag of Madame Payglare, you accepted it gratefully. It was as though the good Père Noël had brought you a charming gift."

He picked up the tickets lying on the table. "Mademoiselle was planning to leave us, I observe. I am not surprised."

Mr. Clutterbuck was still busy with the caramels, but, though toothsome, they did not engage his attention so completely as to prevent him noticing that his hostess had received a shock.

"What's he saying now?" he inquired.

Terry's teeth clicked together.

"He's accusing me of having stolen money from Mrs. Pegler's bag."

"Who's Mrs. Pegler?"

"My former wife," said Old Nick huskily. The explosion of M. Boissonade's bombshell had shaken him to his foundations. "I have been married twice."

"Three times, me," said Russell Clutterbuck. "I don't seem able to keep 'em. Couldn't tell you why. They just melt away. But how did even a Frenchman get a damn-fool notion like that? What makes him think you ever saw the bag? You didn't, did you?"

Terry was honest.

"Yes, I did. I found it. But it was empty. I didn't open it, of course, but I could feel."

Mr. Clutterbuck scratched the lowest of his three chins. He was looking oddly at her through his spectacles.

"Oh, you found the bag?"

"Yes, it was pushed behind the cushion of the chair I was sitting on in the Casino bar. I felt something against my back and reached a hand down——"

"And there was the bag?"

"Yes."

"And you say it was empty?"

"As far as I could tell."

"What does *he* say?"

"He says there were five hundred thousand francs in it."

"Holy mackerel!"

It was at this moment, while Terry stood quivering with fury and praying that it would not turn into a flood of tears, while Old Nick appeared to be trying to swallow something hard and jagged which had stuck in his throat and Russell Clutterbuck was thoughtfully polishing his spectacles, that the door bell rang.

On Commissaire Boissonade the sound had the effect of the last straw. This further addition to the company seemed to him too much. He strode to the door, wrenched it open, glared out and, seeing a young man about to enter, hurled the door in his face. The next moment, Jeff stumbled in, a reddening handkerchief to his nose.

Terry screamed. Old Nick groped for support at a chair. Russell Clutterbuck shrugged his shoulders despairingly, like a man who could have believed practically anything of the French but not this.

"That," he said, "was a silly thing to do. As silly a thing as ever I saw. Frenchmen!" said Russell Clutterbuck, beyond trying to find excuses for the race. "What a set!"

Terry took Jeff's arm and guided him to Kate's bedroom. There was a bathroom there—one of *les derniers conforts* on which the Splendide prided itself—and she indicated it to him. Muttering strange oaths in French, to which language he always returned when stirred, he disappeared, and Terry came back and fixed M. Boissonade with a blazing eye. Then, as if feeling the impossibility of finding words to express herself, she turned and went into the bedroom again.

M. Boissonade watched her go without emotion. He was prepared to wait.

CHAPTER ELEVEN

MR. CLUTTERBUCK stood chewing a pensive cara-mel, a puzzled frown on his face. He was trying to make his mind up. He knew Terry only through occasional meetings during the summer months, but he had formed a high opinion of her and he could not believe her capable of taking a wad of money out of somebody else's handbag. A nice girl like that? Poppycock! She wouldn't dream of doing such a thing. And, anyway, the bag had been empty.

And yet . . . suppose it had not been empty? Suppose she had opened it and seen all that stuff inside it? To a girl in her position, making a scanty living by selling eggs and honey, the sudden discovery of five hundred thousand francs just sitting there waiting to be picked up would have presented a very powerful temptation, and none knew better than he the irresistible force of sudden temptation. There was that time when he had faithfully promised Mrs. Clutterbuck that he would go on a diet, watching his calories like a hawk and cutting out bread, potatoes and all sweets. For two days he had been strong and resolute, but on the third he had lunched at his club—lean chop and spinach—and had seen the waiter bringing the man at the next table a great glistening hillock of strawberry shortcake. And the next thing you knew he was pouring powdered sugar and cream over his own hillock . . . aye, and after that over his second hillock. You never could tell.

It seemed the moment for calling a conference. In the

offices of Winch and Clutterbuck, when anything came up that needed chewing over, a conference was always called. Taking the box of caramels, he drew Old Nick on to the balcony.

"Things don't look so good, Markee," he said.

Old Nick had taken out a cambric handkerchief, one of a set of twelve which he had bought a year ago, if you could call it buying, at the establishment of M. Charvet in Paris, and was dabbing his forehead with it. He, too, was feeling that things did not look good. It is never pleasant for a sensitive man to realize that his sins have found him out, and optimist though he was, skilled in detecting silver linings in the darkest of clouds, he could see in the present crisis no ray of hope.

His was not a high code of ethics . . . indeed, in the course of a chequered career he had frequently been guilty of actions which would have caused a three-card-trick man to purse his lips and shake his head . . . but there were limits to what he could bring himself to do. He was prepared to steal—in what he considered a good cause—but it was impossible for him to stand by unmoved and see a charming girl arrested for the theft. The code of the Maufringneuses, though somewhat shopworn in parts, was rigid on points like that.

"I'm not saying she swiped that dough," proceeded Mr. Clutterbuck, "and I'm not saying she didn't. I'm keeping an open mind. But I'll tell you one thing, and that is that I can't see any jury swallowing that story of hers, however true it is. It wouldn't get past Mrs. Clutterbuck for a moment. No witnesses, nothing but her own word, and the money gone. It's a hell of a situation. As nice a girl as you could wish to meet, but I'm afraid she's going to get it in the neck."

Old Nick applied his handkerchief to his forehead again. "She is innocent, Mr. Clutterbuck!"

"You think so?"

"I know it."

"Well, if you say so. But I doubt if you'll convince the sharecropper."

"The——?"

"I keep thinking of him as a sharecropper. Couldn't tell you why. Something in his manner. The Commissaire or whatever he is. Though it's come as a surprise to me to find that they have commissaires in France. I thought it was only the Russians. Shows how this Communism is spreading."

"I will convince him. Mr. Clutterbuck, I have a confession to make."

Embarking on his story, Old Nick sensed immediately that he had the sympathy of his audience. Mr. Clutterbuck was a broadminded man, difficult to shock.

"I see," he said, having listened with owlish intentness. "You found the money on the floor and pocketed it. Very sensible. I'd have done the same myself. But it leaves you in a spot. What do you plan to do? Confess?"

"Naturally," said Old Nick, looking noble. "What other course is there? But I have a scheme."

"That's good. A scheme is just what we want. What scheme?"

"It is a ruse of which my friend Prince Blamont-Chevry once availed himself with excellent results. One of his creditors—they have always been very numerous—had succeeded in trapping him in his apartment and was threatening, unless he received his money, to send him to prison. Blamont-Chevry, of course, had no money."

"It's often that way."

"But he shrank from the thought of going to prison."

"We all have our likes and dislikes."

"So what did he do? It was useless to plead with the man. He tried it, promising that all should be settled

during the next few days, but the fellow was adamant. He
said that his patience was exhausted and the law must take
its course. Blamont-Chevry drew himself up. He gave
him a haughty look. 'So!' he said. 'I had foreseen this,'
he said, 'and I have made my preparations.' His hand
flickered to his pocket. 'Death rather than dishonour!'
he said, and his hand flew to his mouth. He swallowed.
He tottered. He fell to the floor. The man rushed out,
calling for a doctor, and Blamont-Chevry rose, dusted his
trousers and left by the back door. It was a ruse, you
understand. The fellow thought he had taken poison."

Mr. Clutterbuck stood for a moment in awed silence.
Then he patted Old Nick on the arm.

"You were thinking of trying that one on the Commissaire?" he said gently.

"It would solve everything. I confess. He tells me I
am under arrest. I draw myself up. I say 'Death rather
than dishonour!' I swallow. I totter. I fall. He rushes
from the room, and I drop from the balcony and escape in
my car. I have a car waiting below."

Mr. Clutterbuck patted his arm again. There was a
tender look in his eyes. He was genuinely sorry to be com-
pelled to discourage this naïve soul's simple enthusiasms.
It was, he felt, like telling a child there was no Santa
Claus.

"It wouldn't work," he said. "You wouldn't get to
first base. If you knew as much about cops as I do, you'd
know that they don't rush from rooms. They stick around.
No, we must do better than that. I see your point about
not letting this girl be sent to Devil's Island, or whatever
happens to you in France, when you're the heavy in the
treatment, but you want to use finesse. Here's what I
would suggest. Do a swan dive from the balcony—that
part's all right—and get in your car and drive to Belgium
or somewhere, and leave me to put the facts before the

Commissaire. Then nobody'll have anything to worry about."

Old Nick was staring, spellbound. Some rough indication of the state of his feelings may be given when it is said that at this moment Russell Clutterbuck looked positively beautiful to him.

"Would you?" he whispered.

"Would I what?"

"Tell the Commissaire and—er—attend to everything?"

"Sure."

"It might be advisable to wait some little while."

"To let you make your getaway? Yes, I'll do that."

Old Nick drew a deep breath.

"Are all American publishers like you?" he asked reverently.

"Good God, no," said Russell Clutterbuck, dismissing his confrères in the publishing world with a scornful wave of his caramel. "Most of them haven't enough brains to make a jay bird fly crooked. Want a hand off the balcony?"

"No, thank you," said Old Nick. "I can manage."

2

To be hit on the nose by a door propelled with all the force at his disposal by a muscular commissaire of police can never be a wholly agreeable experience, but there is this to be said in its favour, that it monopolizes the attention and diverts a man temporarily from his other troubles. For some minutes after entering the bathroom, Jeff, giving himself first aid at the cold tap, almost achieved peace of mind. Then, the healing treatment having done its work, his thoughts came back to Terry, to Archie Brice's telephone call, to the shattering news which Archie had so casually imparted, and instantly all the imps that had been prodding him with red-hot pitchforks started prodding him again, assisted by colleagues with white-hot knives and pincers.

That it should have been Terry who had done this to him, that was what bit into him like an acid. Life had brought him into relations with many women, and most of them had not been worth wasting a kiss on—heartless, shallow, grabbing for money, rotten. But this was Terry, frank, open-hearted Terry, Terry of the clear, direct eyes whom he would have sworn incapable of a mercenary thought, Terry who loved him. Yes, he was certain of that, and yet it had needed only the discovery that he was poor to send her into the arms of Freddie Carpenter, the world well lost for money.

It was in a state of cold fury that he had rung the door bell, and it was in a state of cold fury that he now prepared to leave the bathroom. Archie Brice had asked him to interview this girl. He would interview her, he told himself grimly. He would let her see how he despised her. He would be polite, courteous, quite in command of himself, but every word he uttered would be a lash of the whip. Standing there before the mirror, he rehearsed a few of the things he intended to say.

"Good afternoon, Miss Trent."

That would startle her. He could see her staring abashed at this cold, remote stranger with his expressionless face and his aloof 'Good afternoon, Miss Trent'.

"The *Paris Herald-Tribune* have asked me to get a story from you, if you will be kind enough to give me one, about your engagement to Mr. Carpenter. You will understand that anything to do with someone as rich as Mr. Carpenter is news. Readers are always interested in the doings of the rich. Money fascinates them, as it does so many people."

Too subtle? No, just right. And then a lot more along

the same lines, always suave, always courteous, but never without that underlying sting, that icy contempt.

He opened the door and went out, and the first thing he saw was Terry, sitting on Kate's steamer trunk. Her face was in her hands, and she was sobbing.

It was a fiery-eyed Terry Trent who had scorched M. Boissonade with a look and turned and banged the bedroom door behind her, but now reaction had come. Little by little the glow had faded till not even a spark remained, only an awful, creeping fear. She felt trapped and helpless. She looked into a future that held nothing but horror.

Russell Clutterbuck had spoken of the probable reception by a jury of her story of Mrs. Pegler's bag. Cartoons in French papers had left Terry with the impression that they did not have juries in France, and the picture that rose before her mental eye was of a stern-faced *juge d'instruction* who would be much, much harder to convince than twelve kindly jurymen.

He would look at her coldly.

"Accused," he would say . . .

It was at this point that her courage had left her.

Jeff stood in the doorway and felt his heart turn over. There was something so forlorn, so piteous in that crushed, weeping figure on the cabin trunk that all his formidable resolutions were swept away in an instant like leaves on the wind. He looked at her and knew, more certainly than he had ever known anything in his life, that he was not going to be cold and aloof and distant with this girl and—above all—that she was not going to marry Freddie Carpenter. She was going to marry him, Jefferson, Comte d'Escrignon, and anyone who tried to put obstacles in the way would do so at his peril.

But this was not the moment for going into all that. It

could wait. First, she must be soothed and comforted, brought back to her gay self, assured that there was nothing in the world worth crying about like that. He found himself able to move. He went to her and took her gently in his arms.

"*Mon ange, mon trésor, qu'est ce que tu as?*" he said, and for some minutes spoke uninterruptedly in French.

The treatment was effective. She shook herself like a dog coming out of water.

"I'm better now," she said. "Panic's an awful thing."

"Panic? Something has made you afraid? You must not be afraid."

"I can't help it. Why, even Mr. Clutterbuck wasn't sure he believed me. I could see he wasn't."

"I don't understand."

Peremptory knocking sounded on the door. M. Boissonade had grown tired of waiting, and he was boiling with righteous indignation. In all his career, first as a humble *flic* and now as a lordly commissaire, he had never before encountered an accused person who walked off at the tensest point of the inquisition and went into a bedroom and turned the key in the lock. One gets new experiences.

Jeff looked up, surprised.

"What on earth's that?"

"It's the Commissaire. He's going to arrest me."

Jeff took her hand between his and held it.

"Tell me exactly what has been happening," he said.

3

To Mr. Clutterbuck, standing on the balcony and gazing with austere disapproval at the stout bathers on the sands below, eyesores every one of them, there came from the room he had left the sound of a voice speaking vehe-

mently in French. Recognizing it as Jeff's, he frowned a
little. He thought it rather affected of Jeff to be talking
French. Then he realized that he must be addressing his
remarks to the Commissaire, that uneducated oaf who did
not understand English, and absolved him of blame. He
passed through the window, and paused amazed at the
sight of his young friend's nose.

"Gosh!" he said. "That sharecropper certainly swings
a wicked door. You look like W. C. Fields."

Jeff gave him an abstracted glance. There was, Mr.
Clutterbuck now saw, a tenseness about him. It showed itself in his clenched hands, his smouldering eyes and the way
the scar on his face stood out against a cheek that had lost
most of its colour. He looked dangerous, Mr. Clutterbuck
thought, and he was right. Two minutes of M. Boissonade had convinced Jeff that talk was futile and only
action would serve. The interpretation which he placed
on the word action was a liberal one.

"Where's Terry Trent?" asked Mr. Clutterbuck.

"In the bathroom, washing her eyes."

"She been crying?"

"Yes."

"I'm not surprised. And what goes on here?"

"The Commissaire and I have been having an argument.
He thinks she is a thief. I don't. We were discussing it."

"Make any headway?"

"Not much."

"Commissaire kind of set in his views?"

"Yes."

"Then be prepared for tidings of great joy," said Russell
Clutterbuck. "It wasn't Terry Trent who swiped that
dough, it was the Markee."

Jeff stared.

"Told me so himself," Mr. Clutterbuck assured him.
"Took his hair down and came clean only a moment ago.

Hand the news on to the Commissaire. That'll astonish his weak intellect. What a louse the man looks," said Russell Clutterbuck, taking advantage of M. Boissonade's ignorance of the American language to be open and candid.

"A hellhound, every inch of him. Reminds me of an agent I know."

"*Parlez français*," said M. Boissonade.

They ignored him.

"My *father*?" said Jeff.

"That's right. It's a long and interesting story, but no need to go into it now. And if you're thinking that giving him away is going to get him sent up the river, don't worry. He's half-way to Belgium by now, and they can't get at him once he's there. Say, how old is your Dad?"

"How old?" Jeff seemed dazed. "In the sixties."

"I was thinking of the way he hopped off that balcony. Lissom. The only word. Might have been an acrobat. But come on, come on, get action. Tell the Commissaire and watch him wilt."

The stream of French which proceeded from Jeff as he obeyed this instruction sounded all right to Mr. Clutterbuck, as far as that language ever sounded all right to him, but he was concerned to note that it did not seem to be producing the desired effect. So far from wilting, M. Boissonade appeared to be sneering. His lip curled, and he was shrugging his shoulders. Mr. Clutterbuck did not like it.

"Well?" he said.

"He doesn't believe it," said Jeff shortly.

"Doesn't *believe* it?"

"He says a Marquis would never do such a thing."

"The snob! Did you tell him your old man shot off the balcony like a scalded cat and is now rapidly approaching the Belgian frontier?"

"Yes."

"And he still doesn't believe it?"

"No."

Mr. Clutterbuck whistled.

"So what do you do now?"

"What I was just going to do when you came in. I learned a lot of tricks in the Maquis. I shall try a couple on him."

"How do you mean, tricks?"

"Neat ways of putting a man out of action."

Mr. Clutterbuck blinked. This was Mickey Spillane stuff.

"You mean you're going to *slug* him?"

"And tie him up." Jeff gave the publisher a searching look. His acquaintance with Russell Clutterbuck had been brief, and he had no means of knowing how the other stood on these matters. He might conceivably feel it his duty as a citizen to interfere. "You haven't any objection?" he said, narrowing his gaze.

"None," said Mr. Clutterbuck hastily. "None whatever. What do you do after that?"

"I take Terry and we catch the plane for America. She's got the tickets."

"Going to America, eh? You might look Mrs. Clutterbuck up."

"Certainly."

"You won't be able to see her because of her mumps, but you can shout Hello through the door."

"Delighted. I'll bring my wife along."

"You told me you weren't married."

"I shall be by that time."

"You mean Terry Trent?"

"My dear Russ, is there anybody else any sane man could possibly consider marrying?"

"Well, that's fine. Nice girl."

"That's how she strikes me."

"*Parlez FRANCAIS!*" bellowed M. Boissonade.

Mr. Clutterbuck gave him a friendly smile, waving his hand as much as to say that all would come right in the future. Then his face became grave again.

"This Macky stuff," he said dubiously. "You think it would work?"

"It has been tried and tested."

"He's pretty big."

"I've handled bigger."

Mr. Clutterbuck hastened to dispel any idea that he was trying to discourage him.

"Don't get me wrong, I'm all in favour of his getting knocked cold," he said cordially. "I don't think I ever saw a guy that needed getting knocked cold more. No, not even some of those authors of mine. The only thing I was wondering was wouldn't it be better to try something else first?"

"If you have any suggestions?"

"Well, it seems to me that what's needed here is tact."

"Tact?"

"It's like what that barman was telling me, the one that came from my home town. That's kind of a tough joint he's in, and he was saying how often, especially on Saturday nights, the customers get above themselves and start throwing their weight around. He said he always found he got the best results by using tact. The first move in my opinion is to mellow the man with drink. You know how different everything looks to you after you've tucked a few under your belt. I wouldn't be at all surprised if a glass or two of that champagne over there didn't act like a charm on the fellow."

Jeff was not enthusiastic. Mr. Clutterbuck seemed to him, as Old Nick had seemed to Mr. Clutterbuck, a naïve optimist vainly chasing rainbows. He could not see M. Boissonade melting under the influence of even a magnum of champagne.

"Try it if you like," he said indifferently.

"Try everything once," said Mr. Clutterbuck. "That's my motto."

He waddled over to the table, poured out a glass and bore it to where the Commissaire sat, his arms folded, his face inflexible.

"A spot, moose-yer?" he said winningly. "It's on the house."

M. Boissonade was surprised. Early in the preceedings he had observed the champagne—a detective notices everything—but he had entertained no hope of ever being offered any of it. A pleased look came into his face, and his prejudice against Americans waned for the first time in years. He took the glass and sipped genteelly. Then, as if feeling that this was no time for half-measures, he drained the beaker to the last drop, and Mr. Clutterbuck took it back to the table and refilled it.

Jeff was eyeing the love-feast sourly.

"It won't be any good," he said.

"You don't think he'll soften?"

"No."

"Well, watch him after this one," said Mr. Clutterbuck, waddling back to the Commissaire. "It's got a Mickey Finn in it."

Jeff gave a gasp. He saw that he had underestimated the resourcefulness of this pearl among publishers. It was always thus. Hotheaded Youth thought in terms of crude violence. Its wiser elders knew that there were other simpler ways.

"That barman from my home town slipped me a couple last night. He said you never knew when they might not come in useful, and it was his opinion that no man should be without them. When you are as old as I am," said Mr. Clutterbuck, moralizing, "you'll know that there's practically no dilemma in this world that a

Mickey Finn can't solve. If I had my way, every child
in the land——"

He broke off. With a suggestion in his manner of
one who has been struck by lightning, Pierre Alexandre
Boissonade was sliding from his chair, and as he nestled on
the floor, patently off the active list for a long time to come,
Mr. Clutterbuck gave a satisfied nod, the sort of nod
Michelangelo might have given on completing a master-
piece.

"Didn't I tell you?" he said. "Tact. There's nothing
like it."

He would have spoken further and probably made some
observations of great value, but at this moment the telephone rang and he leaped to it, the good husband all eager-
ness to hear his wife's voice.

"Hello? . . . Yes? . . . What? . . . Oh, HELLO,
honey, how are you, honey . . . You *what*? You tried all
last night to get me at the Ritz? But I'm not in Paris,
honey, I'm at a place on the coast called Roville. I had to
come down here to confer with a young fellow whose book
I'm doing. We left Paris after lunch yesterday, that's why
you couldn't reach me, honey."

Out of the corner of his eye he saw Terry come in, and
waved a fatherly hand in her direction.

"Good-bye, Russ," said Jeff.

"Good-bye, Mr. Clutterbuck," said Terry.

"Good-bye. See you on the other side, Jeff. Eh?"
said Mr. Clutterbuck, once more addressing Mrs. Clutterbuck. "Why am I calling you Jeff? I'm not calling you
Jeff, honey, I was speaking to the young fellow I was
telling you about." He looked over his shoulder. The
door had closed. He was alone. "Say, listen, honey," he
said. "Who do you think I've run into here? You know
those Trent girls who sell us honey, honey. I'm talking
from their suite at the Hotel Splendide where I spent last

night. Remember the one they call Terry? She's marrying this young fellow whose book I'm doing. He's the Comte d'Escrignon, and his father's the Markee de-something—I've-forgotten. They're flying to America this afternoon, and I've told them to look you up and . . ." He looked over his shoulder at the opening door. "I'll have to ring off now, honey. Another of those Trent girls has just come in, and I'll have to explain to her why there's a commissaire of police having fits on the floor. Good-bye, honey, I'll give you a buzz later."

He replaced the receiver, adjusted his spectacles and prepared to make the facts in the case of Pierre Alexandre Boissonade clear to Kate, who he could see was a little puzzled about it all.

CHAPTER TWELVE

IN a form-fitting swivel chair in his office on Madison Avenue Mr. Clutterbuck sat waiting for Terry, whom he was taking to lunch.

The nine months which had passed since his notable display of tact at the Hotel Splendide in Roville-sur-Mer had enlarged the publisher's waistline by several inches, and Terry as she came in regarded him with awe. She wondered how he did it. Shakespeare, had he been present, would have felt the same. 'Upon what meat doth this our Clutterbuck feed that he is grown so great?' he would have asked himself.

"Watch that figure, Russ," she said maternally.

"Never mind my figure," Mr. Clutterbuck replied with a touch of pique. "You're late."

"Only a minute or two. I was talking to Jeff on the phone. He's in Boston with the play."

"How's it doing?"

"It seems to be a hit there."

"And I'll bet it's a hit in New York. That's how it goes," said Mr. Clutterbuck broodingly. "There's no justice in the world. I work myself to a skeleton for thirty years, giving the business my all, and what do I get? A bare living. This boy of yours dashes off a novel in a couple of weeks, Sam Behrman turns it into a play in another couple of weeks, and if it runs for two years, as it probably will, he'll get four hundred thousand dollars for the picture rights."

"He won't get it all."

"He'll get quite enough. More than enough. Authors are the only guys that make any money in this game. Nothing in it for the publishers. One of these days you'll see me selling pencils in the street. If I can afford to buy any pencils."

Terry patted his bald head.

"This is not the true Russell Clutterbuck speaking," she said. "I can see what's the matter with you, my poor lamb. Subconsciously, without knowing it, you want your lunch. The trouble with you, Russ, is that you're so spiritual, you don't realize that you have to eat. Left to yourself, you would just sit here sniffing a rose and thinking beautiful thoughts. Where are you taking me? Make it somewhere good. You can knock it off your income tax under the head of Entertainment."

"We're going to the Mazarin. Best place in town. I'm a shareholder. Come on, come on, come on! Are you planning to keep me hanging around here all day? That's what's wrong with women. They dally. They loiter. Mrs. Clutterbuck's the same. And that reminds me. Can you think of a good story that'll cover my being out all night tomorrow? I mean something that'll get by with Mrs. Clutterbuck."

"Sorry, no."

"I'll have to consult Jeff. Where is he in Boston? At the Ritz? I'll call him up during lunch. There's a big poker game on tomorrow night, and I ought to be there, and there's no sense in sitting in on a poker game unless you're able to carry on till breakfast-time next morning. Jeff will think up something. I have every confidence in Jeff. How that boy ever came to be a Frenchman beats me."

"What's wrong with Frenchmen?"

"They talk French. And they wear beards."

"Jeff doesn't."

"No," said Mr. Clutterbuck, for he was a fairminded man, "he doesn't, that's right.   Never know when he may not start, though.   You miss him, I shouldn't wonder?"

Terry's eyes moistened.

"Every minute.   You know that poem about the woman wailing for her demon lover."

"No, I don't."

"Then you ought to. Don't publishers ever read anything?"

"Not more than they have to."

"Well, anyway, that's me."

"So you're still liking marriage?"

"It's the only life."

"Too early to say that after . . . how long is it?"

"Eight months, three weeks and two days, and it isn't a bit too early. It's heaven, Russ, and getting more heavenly all the time. I can't speak of marriage too highly."

"Lots to be said for it, of course, and on the other hand, plenty to be said against it.   You wait till he gets chicken-pox."

It seemed to Terry that a cog had worked loose in the conversation.

"Chickenpox?"

"It upsets the home. Mrs. Clutterbuck's got chicken-pox."

"No?"

"Pink spots all over her."

"But it seems only yesterday that she had mumps?"

"It was only yesterday that she had mumps."

"She does seem to have everything, doesn't she?"

"That's right.   If it's going, Mrs. Clutterbuck gets it. She's had measles twice."

"I didn't know you could get measles twice."

"She managed it. Now for the last time," said Mr. Clutterbuck with quiet menace. "Are you coming or are you not?"

The Mazarin was one of those ornate restaurants which abound in the side streets between Madison and Park Avenues. It was evidently doing well. At first glance every table appeared to be occupied, but one in the most desirable corner was found for Mr. Clutterbuck, who seemed to be a valued client. His entry started something in the nature of a civic reception, with waiters rushing from every side to minister to his needs. Presently the mob of admirers and supporters thinned, and they began their meal.

It was never immediately that a lunch with Russell Clutterbuck became a feast of reason and a flow of soul, for when restoring his tissues he believed in rigid concentration, but eventually the moment arrived when he felt at liberty to converse.

"Well, young Terry Trent," he said.

"Well, boss."

"What I was saying just now about publishers and authors," said Mr. Clutterbuck, returning to the subject on which he had touched at his office. He appeared to have been brooding on it. "Winch and Clutterbuck published that book of your young man's. Why aren't we in on the play? The whole question of subsidiary rights is one that will have to be gone into and thoroughly threshed out."

"Go on, grind the face of the poor."

"Poor! There isn't an author on our list that isn't richer than I am. Who winters in Florida? The author. Whose limousine splashes the publisher with mud as he waits for his bus? The author's. Look at that boy of yours. Pulling the stuff in in handfuls. I suppose he's feeling on top of the world these days?"

"Well, he's very pleased at the way the book has gone——"

"Good publishers. The answer every time."

"—and about that play, of course——"

"Subsidiary rights. We'll get 'em some day."

"—but, as a matter of fact, he's rather worried."

"What's he got to be worried about?"

"His father."

"The Markee?"

"Yes, he's wondering if he's all right."

"Tell him to relax. The Markee's doing fine."

"How do you know? Have you heard from him?"

"And seen him. I see him right along."

Terry stared.

"You mean he's here? Here in New York?"

"Sure."

"Why didn't you let us know? Didn't you tell him where we were?"

"Certainly, and he said he'd look you up as soon as he could get around to it. He's only been here a week, and he's been busy."

Terry looked thoughtful.

"It's going to be awkward meeting him. I shall feel like John took me round to see his mother."

"You'll feel what?"

"Don't you know the old song?"

"No."

"You don't seem to know anything. Father used to sing it. It's about a girl who gets engaged to a man and he takes her round to see his mother and the mother looks at her and shakes her head and says 'Poor John! Poor John!'"

"Who's John?"

"Oh, Russ! You're stupefied with food. I mean, the Marquis is going to take a dim view of his son marrying someone without any money."

"He's in no position to criticize. His wife hasn't a bean."

"His what? He's not married?"

"Certainly he's married. Been married for more than a month. I ought to have told you that. Slipped my mind, I guess. She's a nice woman. French, I grant you, but I suppose somebody has to be. She was a cook."

"A *cook*?"

"And a darned good cook, too. I've had a couple of her dinners. Ah, there he is," said Mr. Clutterbuck. "There's the old Markee."

Terry's eyes flitted about the room.

"Where? I don't see him."

"At the table over there where the waiter's helping the guy to minced capon with poached egg. Sorry now I didn't have some of that. It looks good."

Terry gave a gasp. She had seen the tall, slim, elegant figure at which he was pointing.

"The head waiter!"

"That's right, and a good one. I had him taped the first time I saw him. I've an unerring gift that way. 'The perfect head waiter,' I said to myself. Look what he's got . . . style, manner, dignity, everything. So when he wrote to me and said that what with one thing and another he was coming pretty near the end of that money he'd borrowed from his former wife and could I get him a job in New York, I wrote back Sure. I knew he couldn't miss. Of course, he had to study first. You can't be a head waiter if you don't study. I placed him at a hotel down in Florida and told him to start learning the business."

"And that's where he met the cook?"

"That's where. She was working for some rich people who had a house there, and they sat next to each other one night at the pictures. Love at first sight it was, or anyway as soon as he had tasted one of her ragouts. He clocked in here at the Mazarin a week ago, and was a riot from the start, as I knew he would be. He's got . . . what is it that Frenchmen have?"

"Beards?"

"No, not beards."

"You said they had beards."

"Yes, but this is something else. Begins with a journey. Ha!" said Mr. Clutterbuck, memory returning to its throne. "Journey say quar. He's got journey say quar. So Jeff can stop worrying about the Markee, he's in. With all the tips he gets he must be coining money. Head waiters always do. It's only the poor fat-headed publishers that end up selling apples in the street."

"Pencils, you said."

"Pencils or apples, doesn't matter which. I wish I'd had the sense to be a head waiter."

"You haven't the figure."

"I don't want any more of your cracks about my figure. You leave my figure alone, and it'll leave you alone. And your Jeff's going to look just like me five years from now."

"He isn't!"

"You wait."

Terry followed Old Nick with a fascinated eye as he moved to and fro on his professional duties. Russell Clutterbuck was right. He had style, manner, dignity and all the other qualities that make for success in the walk in life which he had chosen. Into the simple act of whipping off a dish cover and letting a customer get a look at an order of roast chicken garnished with mushrooms, he seemed to infuse a suggestion of the plenipotentiary of some proud country presenting his credentials to a reigning monarch. He was the head waiter to end all head waiters.

It seemed to her, as he approached their table, that there was a gravity, a purposefulness about him which she had not observed in the old Roville days. His eyes widened a little as he saw her, but he gave no other indication of emotion.

"Everything satisfactory, I trust, Mr. Clutterbuck?"

"Fine."

"Madame," said Old Nick, with a courtly bow of just the right depth.

There was something so remote, so majestic, about this new Old Nick that Terry found herself at a loss for small talk. Mr. Clutterbuck, busy digesting, apparently had no intention of contributing anything. He was sitting back in his chair, breathing gently, a rather glassy look in his eyes.

"Yours must be very interesting work," she said.

"Exceedingly, Madame."

"Mr. Clutterbuck says he would like to be a head waiter."

"Indeed, Madame?"

"But I tell him——"

"Never mind what you tell me," said Mr. Clutterbuck, coming to life. He heaved himself up. "Order coffee, while I go and phone that husband of yours."

"Psst! Psst!" hissed Old Nick, attracting the attention of the waiter. "*Le Café. Vite.*"

With the departure of Mr. Clutterbuck things magically became easier. Old Nick did not smile, but there crept into his eye a friendly gleam which encouraged Terry. She fancied that she observed in it a touch of Auld Lang Syne.

"Jeff's up in Boston," she said.

"Ah, yes?"

"With the play they've made of his book."

"Ah, yes?"

"Everyone seems to think he's going to make a fortune out of it."

The gleam in Old Nick's eye became more pronounced.

A head waiter makes good money, but he can always do with a devoted son who pays surtax.

"So everything's fine," said Terry. "Mr. Clutterbuck tells me you're married, too? I'm sure you're very happy."

"Exceedingly, Madame. The Marquise is a very remarkable woman."

"You took a chance, didn't you, like Jeff and me?"

"Madame?"

"I wish you wouldn't call me Madame. Terry is the name."

A touch of its former frostiness returned to Old Nick's manner. He seemed shocked at the suggestion that he should address a client as Terry. Later, perhaps, but not now.

"A chance, you were saying, Madame?"

"Well, we all got married without having any money."

Old Nick quivered. She had brought up a subject on which he felt deeply. The man of sensibility replaced the head waiter.

"Money!" he said, and you could see he despised the stuff. "It is not money that matters, it is love. Lovers need not be afraid of being poor. I remember saying that once to my son Jafe. 'If you are poor, Jafe, and married to the woman you love,' I said, 'everything becomes an adventure. A new hat for her is an achievement. The dreams, the plans, the obstacles that must be surmounted— the rich don't have any of that.' There can be no castles in the air for people who live in castles. One room up six flights of stairs," proceeded Old Nick, gathering momentum, "what more do lovers need? When you blow out the candle beside the bed and the dark closes about you, you can make believe that you are in a room at Versailles, with silk hangings and cupids dancing on the ceiling."

Terry said "Oh?" It seemed all that there was to say.

"Love and hard work," said Old Nick. "That is the secret."

"I suppose the work is hard?"

"Zut!" said Old Nick. He did not often say 'Zut', but this was a special occasion. "I welcome it. Love and hard work, those are the two things that make life worth living. I have always said so, always."

He broke off to allow the waiter with the coffee access to the table. The waiter, an elderly man of rather battered appearance, who seemed nervous under Old Nick's eye, filled her cup and went on pouring. A brown sea darkened the tablecloth, and Old Nick burst into a torrent of French so rapid that Terry could not follow it. From the fact that the waiter vanished as if shot from a gun she deduced that he had been dispatched in quest of a new cloth.

"A thousand apologies," said Old Nick. "A new waiter, not yet accustomed to his duties. I engaged him out of charity. It was weak of me, but he is an old friend, the Prince Blamont-Chevry. He has much to learn, a great deal to learn."

He passed away discreetly. Mr. Clutterbuck was rolling up to the table.

Mr. Clutterbuck seemed annoyed.

"Did you get Jeff?" said Terry.

"I got him. The young reptile."

"Mr. Clutterbuck, you are speaking of the man I love."

The publisher sat down heavily.

"Do you know what that young hound said to me?" he asked.

"What?"

"He told me I ought to be ashamed of myself, leaving Mrs. Clutterbuck on her sick-bed and going off playing poker. He flatly refused to help me. 'Stay at her side,' he said, 'and tell her funny stories. Sing to her. Dance before her. Be a prop and comfort to her at least till the pink spots have disappeared,' he said. 'Strive to be a model husband like me,' he said."

"He's a baa-lamb."

"Who's a baa-lamb?"

"Jeff's a baa-lamb."

"He's a nothing of the kind. He's a wash-out and a broken reed. I class him with the Commissaire. You were a chump to marry a man like that, Terry Trent. Still, I suppose you girls have got to take what you can get these days."

"That's it," said Terry.

READ MORE IN PENGUIN

In every corner of the world, on every subject under the sun, Penguin represents quality and variety – the very best in publishing today.

For complete information about books available from Penguin – including Puffins, Penguin Classics and Arkana – and how to order them, write to us at the appropriate address below. Please note that for copyright reasons the selection of books varies from country to country.

In the United Kingdom: Please write to *Dept. EP, Penguin Books Ltd, Bath Road, Harmondsworth, West Drayton, Middlesex UB7 ODA*

In the United States: Please write to *Consumer Sales, Penguin USA, P.O. Box 999, Dept. 17109, Bergenfield, New Jersey 07621-0120*. VISA and MasterCard holders call 1-800-253-6476 to order Penguin titles

In Canada: Please write to *Penguin Books Canada Ltd, 10 Alcorn Avenue, Suite 300, Toronto, Ontario M4V 3B2*

In Australia: Please write to *Penguin Books Australia Ltd, P.O. Box 257, Ringwood, Victoria 3134*

In New Zealand: Please write to *Penguin Books (NZ) Ltd, Private Bag 102902, North Shore Mail Centre, Auckland 10*

In India: Please write to *Penguin Books India Pvt Ltd, 706 Eros Apartments, 56 Nehru Place, New Delhi 110 019*

In the Netherlands: Please write to *Penguin Books Netherlands bv, Postbus 3507, NL-1001 AH Amsterdam*

In Germany: Please write to *Penguin Books Deutschland GmbH, Metzlerstrasse 26, 60594 Frankfurt am Main*

In Spain: Please write to *Penguin Books S. A., Bravo Murillo 19, 1° B, 28015 Madrid*

In Italy: Please write to *Penguin Italia s.r.l., Via Felice Casati 20, I–20124 Milano*

In France: Please write to *Penguin France S. A., 17 rue Lejeune, F–31000 Toulouse*

In Japan: Please write to *Penguin Books Japan, Ishikiribashi Building, 2–5–4, Suido, Bunkyo-ku, Tokyo 112*

In Greece: Please write to *Penguin Hellas Ltd, Dimocritou 3, GR–106 71 Athens*

In South Africa: Please write to *Longman Penguin Southern Africa (Pty) Ltd, Private Bag X08, Bertsham 2013*

BY THE SAME AUTHOR

Life at Blandings
**Full Moon   Galahad at Blandings   Heavy Weather
A Pelican at Blandings   Pigs Have Wings
Service with a Smile   Something Fresh
Summer Lightning   Sunset at Blandings
Uncle Fred in the Springtime**
and the omnibus editions
**Life at Blandings   Imperial Blandings
Lord Emsworth Acts for the Best**

Short Stories
**Blandings Castle   Lord Emsworth and Others
Eggs, Beans and Crumpets   The Man with Two Left Feet
The Man Upstairs and Other Stories
The Gold Bat and Other School Stories
The Pothunters and Other School Stories**

The Mike and Psmith Books
**Mike at Wrykyn   Mike and Psmith
Leave it to Psmith   Psmith in the City   Psmith, Journalist**
and the omnibus
The World of Psmith

and
**The Adventures of Sally   Bachelors Anonymous
Big Money   Cocktail Time   Company for Henry
A Damsel in Distress   Do Butlers Burgle Banks?
Doctor Sally   A Gentleman of Leisure
The Girl in Blue   Hot Water   If I Were You
The Indiscretions of Archie   Laughing Gas   The Little Nugget
The Luck of the Bodkins   Money in the Bank   Money for Nothing
Pearls, Girls and Monty Bodkin   Piccadilly Jim
Quick Service   Sam the Sudden   The Small Bachelor
Spring Fever   Summer Moonshine   Ukridge
Uncle Fred: An Omnibus   Uncle Dynamite
Uneasy Money   Young Men in Spats**

also published
Wodehouse on Wodehouse   Yours, Plum